INSIDE MY MIND
VOLUME II

INSIDE MY MIND: VOLUME II
DOUGLAS OWEN

Science Fiction and Fantasy Publications
HTTPS://SCIFIFANTASYPUBLICATIONS.COM
An imprint of DAOwen Publications

INSIDE MY MIND: VOLUME II / Douglas Owen

ISBN 978-1-928094-29-6
EISBN 978-1-928094-30-2

Volume I edited by MJ Moores

Cover art by MMT Productions

10 9 8 7 6 5 4 3 2 1

Acknowledgements

There are so many people I need to thank in the creation of this book. They are friends, acquaintances, and loved ones. Each had a small or large part in making this collection come to life.

For my family who have always been behind me in my adventures in writing and publishing. I cannot express my love for all of you. Without your backing, none of this would happen.

To my writing friends, they are always telling me to keep pushing the stories out, and celebrating my winning streaks when they happen. All of you are an unbelievable supportive group that I am more than happy to be a part of.

My test readers and critiquing partners, I hope your brains did not explode while putting me through the demands for perfection. It is you who help push my writing to the next level.

To my editor friend, MJ, you really do know how to push a writer to their best when it comes to suggestions. Thanks for all the help.

And finally, to my wife for sticking through all the silent nights of me typing away, this one is for you.

The Stories

The Flash

Sneak Peek

GOT ONE

Bill enjoyed the deep greens and browns of the thick forest. The mixture of trees dazzled with life. The fresh scent of rain took away the remaining buzz of the office that always echoes in his mind. Bill's spirit lifted at the sound of the bolt sliding across the breech. He smiled, and released a breath. His rushing heart slowed. He anticipated a call from the office sometime soon, a weak show of concern about where he was and the other missing co-workers.

A branch rustled to his left. He lifted the Savage 10/100 and sighted down the scope. Dew dripped from newly born leaves. Fog covered the scope aperture. He cursed under his breath. The salesman was right: cheaping out on such an important part of the hunt was a mistake…

Dizziness took hold of Bill as he stared down at the scope display case, a thousand questions raced through his mind. Sounds of muffled gun fire bounced in the weapon shop's showroom. The conglomeration of simple pistol sights to sniper scopes staggered his already fuzzy mind. One hand pressed against the case to help support his weight while the other held that special piece of paper every Canadian needed in order to own a firearm: a permit costing over $800.

He had studied for three months, took classes every Saturday, and finally wrote the tests, but he could now purchase and carry a weapon of his choice—from his home to a range, or into the wilderness for hunting. The anal-retentive laws supposedly made it safe for people to live, but he knew all it did was keep a form of recreation out of the hands of the masses. If you really wanted a gun or rifle, you could get one. At least those were the words from his instructor, said while scanning the room waiting for someone to take the bait, ask a question, or just up and leave, looking for the fast out to their problem: how to get a weapon to kill someone.

He wanted to leave, to take the easy way.

No one left the first day.

Bill filled everything out meticulously; his I's dotted with the exact same distance from the body and T's crossed at the correct height. He presented his papers to the police, and waited. The police check on his background found nothing out of the ordinary.

Reality snapped back to him as a young, heavy-set man approached from behind the counter. His long, straight, black hair clung to the sides of his head, gathered behind his neck in a loose ponytail, and splayed out to the mid of his back. A pre-pubescent beard, more sparse than full, adorned his chin, partially grown on pudgy cheeks. Nothing could have grown on his neck, for he had none, just a slab of fat gathered there to keep the head from falling forward.

"Can I help you?" the rotund man asked, pressing his stomach against the display.

Bill raised a hand to his nose, almost recoiling at the obscenity of the man's coffee and cigarette breath and body odor. Another person who failed to clean himself properly. A lingering of gun oil followed the salesman, along with the musk Bill always experienced around the grossly obese. Bill imagined dried sweat and soil clinging to the unreachable areas of the man's body. He looked down and noticed the man held out a meaty paw, nails too long for hygiene, and dirt crusted under them. Bill wondered what to do about this impossible situation. He took the high road and put hands behind his back.

"I-I-I'm looking for a s-s-scope," Bill stuttered.

The salesperson withdrew his pre-offered hand. "What'cha hunting?"

Bill raised his gaze, past the protruding belly, mustard stain, crumbs on chin, and saw two brown eyes staring back at him waiting for a response.

"Because if you're lookin' to kill someone that be in the section over there." The man raised his flabby arm, displaying the bumps of several

2

cysts.

Bill flushed, numbness creeping over his extremities, before he recognized the direction the salesman pointed. The exit.

"N-n-n-no ... not people." He scrambled for something, pain exploding inside. This was the longest he'd talked to anyone in a year. "B-b-bears."

The salesman nodded. "What'cha mounting it on?"

How much did he want to tell this man? "A-a-a Savage 10/100."

The salesman whistled. "Nice rifle." He produced a set of keys out of a too tight pocket. "What's your range?"

Bill kept his gaze on the counter as the man pulled out groups of sights. He stopped at 10.

"A-a-about fifty to a hundred f-f-feet."

The salesman's hand stopped midway in placing a scope down. The pause became uncomfortable, then the man chuckled. "Funny guy." He continued to stack sights. "Okay, you have a choice here, but I need ta know the price range you want to spend."

Bill scratched the back of his head, thoughts of his bank balance, upcoming bills, and how much he needed for gas that week scrambled for attention. "I d-d-don't know, how about s-s-showing me what would be g-g-good?"

The salesman explained each scope, plusses and minuses, costs and savings. How disappointing a hunt would be with this person huffing and pubbing to keep up, his scent scaring away all the animals for miles.

The sound of an animal pushing through the dense underbrush of the forest in the distance caught Bill's attention, but he couldn't see it in the early morning light. The breaking of twigs, rustle of leaves, the occasional grunt. A big animal. And even with the morning light at his back, he couldn't make out exactly where the noise came from.

The tree was his best bet. Scouting out the terrain took him a month. He'd spent it putting down bacon grease, meat fat, stale bread, and other things animals liked. A blind twenty feet up a solid birch tree took two days to build. Animals rarely looked up. They just trudged through the forest foraging. Nothing came out of the brush for him to shoot at.

He sat back down, removed the lid from his cup, and poured more coffee from the thermos, disappointed no more steam wafted from the container. It was going to be a long day.

Pete stood over Bill, glaring at either the keyboard or monitor; which one, Bill could not tell. The florescent lights of the office flickered, casting a changing shadow on the desk. Pete's full head of hair, with no grey, gelled in little wavy spikes. His close-trimmed beard, still not fully formed, reminded everyone of his early success in the company.

The closeness was enough to make sweat run down Bill's back. His boss usually sent him emails and told him what he needed, waiting for the return of work, which happened fast. But lately, the problems were more complex, needing further insight into the programming. When Bill emailed a question, Pete came over, instead of just responding.

"I need to understand what you're looking at." Pete's breath reeked of decaying garbage left in the sun.

Bill motioned to the screen. "H-h-here." He hoped that would be all he needed to say to the man. The less he spoke, the less chance to smell the rank breath.

"What code are we looking at?" Pete leaned forward a little more, his breath filling Bill's personal space, making it the only stench he could smell.

"T-t-there," Bill replied. He swallowed, turned his head, and almost gasped. Then he used the mouse to highlight the abnormality. "T-t-the code t-t-tells the system t-t-to start a p-p-password recovery every f-f-four years. T-t-the certificate expires. T-t-this code stops it from autom-m-matically recovering." Sweat ran down his forehead.

"Oh, is that all?" Pete straightened.

"B-b-but this could h-h-have a n-n-negative effect on t-t-the c-c-customer's experience. C-c-cause lots of c-c-calls to our h-h-help d-d-desk for s-s-support." He swiveled his chair. Pete stared at him with that look. The one normal people give to those with society issues. Disdain, criticism, even laughter behind his eyes.

As quickly as Bill caught the glare, Pete's face went flaccid, hiding any emotional contempt it displayed earlier. "I wouldn't worry about that. It's not our department. All we're testing is the code change sent in by the programmers." He pivoted, started to walk away then stopped. "Oh, there's a team building exercise later next month. Some exec thought it would be good to get all us geeks out into the forest for a quick game of capture the flag." He looked over his shoulder. "It's mandatory."

Bill drove, glancing between the road and fuel gage, coffee cup in a holder, a half-eaten sandwich in a container discarded on the seat beside him. Why he packed peanut butter and grape jelly was beyond him, maybe the excitement for the events to come. But he needed something to keep his body going when he woke so early, and that was the easiest thing to make. His old Jimmy ate gas faster than he could pump it in, but the thing could drive through a brick wall. His spine rolled with all the bumps the big truck went over.

His phone's GPS told him to proceed further North on 144, until he hit a road called 661, which led to a small town called Gogama. Flag's Ahoy, the company running the retreat, headquartered there. Arrival time was set for 10 am next Saturday, but he drove there today, Tuesday, having taken a day off. Maps lay strewn on the floor of the Jimmy, showing overhead shots and people having fun running around in the forest.

The retreat offered guided hikes and fully catered BBQs afterward, but his company had cheaped out, telling everyone to bring something for a potluck, saying it would build the team knowing they needed to supply food for one another. Bill hated to eat food prepared by others. Unclean hands and dirt under fingernails carried diseases.

A quick trip into the deep forest would be the last civilized thing they would do all day. And the company used a Deuce-and-a-half to get the people in and out. The old train tracks crossing Minisinakwa Lake were key. Fortunately, his truck sported the off-road suspension to haul his boat out of the water. He slapped his forehead. "I c-c-could have b-b-brought the boat and f-f-fished today."

Emails flew back and forth about the upcoming event, each questioning what the other would bring. Bill read every one and ticked off a list of people bringing different food. He came across a company email, for a modest fee, offering to book cabins at the lodge just outside town. He pulled up the resort website and compared. The fee showed no group discount, and he phoned them to book a spot for his trip north earlier that week. The webpage link took him to the area map; he studied it once again, and a smile crossed his lips ever so slightly.

Friday, 4 pm and everyone in the office rushed for the door. Bill held back, waiting for the throng to trample out of the building. The mindless escape only to have hours of driving loom over them. This spring day promised to carry over to the next. He waited, and when the last of the milling crowd gathered outside and migrated to their cars, he stood, knees popping loudly, and put on his spring jacket.

"Thought you would have left by now." Pete strutted over to his desk, a bundle of files under his arm. "You in a rush?"

Bill glanced at the time, the phone on the desk blinking a reminder of his set departure time for the camp. "N-n-no."

"Good." Pete dropped the five files on his desk. "We need the code analysed on these five projects, fast." He smiled. "Nothing like a little overtime to get you rolling on the big adventure, right?" He slapped Bill's back.

Bill's vision fogged, then cleared. He frowned and kicked Pete in the testacies. The man crumpled, grasping between his legs. The pained look on his reddened face gave Bill a perverse pleasure as he watched his supervisor roll on the floor in agony.

Fingers snapped in front of him and the world came back into focus. "Earth to Bill." Pete stopped the action of his fingers. "You good with this?"

"Y-y-yes." Bill swivelled his seat back to the monitor and pulled up the code.

Bill pinched the bridge of his nose, hit the enter key, and switched off the computer. Three hours. He glanced at his watch, behind schedule. He pushed away from the desk, stood, and hustled outside. At his truck, he dropped his keys several times, trying to unlock the vehicle. Frustrated, he finally opened the door, jumped in, and headed north in the weekend traffic. He might even be able to stop off at the apartment to grab something to eat and the cooler filled with supplies. With a little luck, he'd be in the woods before sunset. Bile rose up his throat at the thought of being late to the campground and getting lost in the woods.

The sun cast eerie shadows across the road. Bill pushed the Jimmy harder to make up the time, but the faster he went the worse the gas mileage became. He estimated 16 litres per 100 kilometres at his break-neck speed of 130 KMH. The shadows kept lengthening.

Darkness spread across the small town, and only the lights of the fishing camp glowed in the background. He could say a number of things about the Northern towns, but a thriving nightlife was not one of them. After parking the truck, he made a quick run into the camp office, hoping to secure a room. An old woman before him ran a gnarled finger down a list, tisking as she went.

"Should have called ahead," she said, voice a gravel pit and breath full of cigarettes. "We could have put something aside for ya."

"I d-d-didn't t-t-think of t-t-that," Bill gasped out the sentence.

The old woman stopped, her finger hovering over the lines of names and room numbers for a second. "Are you okay?" Her tone more accusatory than anything. "The cops don't like drunk drivers around here. Too many Indians doing it."

With heating cheeks, Bill shook his head. "N-n-not d-d-drinking, j-j-just t-t-tired."

"You sure?" The woman did not continue searching.

"J-j-just a r-r-room, p-p-please."

Light streamed in Bill's room. He opened an eye and stared at the clock. 6 am. Ignoring the stomach pains from not eating, he jumped into his truck and drove through the town of Gogama, across Minisinakwa Lake. The old railroad bridge jarred his kidneys. Finally, he made it to the hunting blind he'd set up a few days prior. He climbed up, holding a rope end, then hoisted up the rifle, cooler, and field glasses. Once they were secure, he climbed down and retraced his tracks back to the lodge, just in time for the 9 am breakfast.

Bill swallowed the last of his pancakes as a young man jumped up on a bench, whistled and waved both arms high.

"Hello everyone!" The man held his arms out wide. "I'd like to welcome y'all to our Capture the Flag team building day. Hope everyone slept well."

Bill glanced around, pulled his cap down to hide his red eyes, but no one looked his way. No one ever did.

"I'd like to go over some ground rules and safety instructions before we head out." The young man explained how far the trip into the wilderness would be and how to call for help using the small whistles

7

each of them carried. "And finally, we'll be giving everyone these vests with a big orange dot on the front and back." He held one up for everyone body to see. "Don't remove them. Hunters may be out this weekend, and they will not shoot at orange."

The corner of Bill's mouth pulled back and up.

Pete climbed into the back of the Deuce-and-a-half and sat next to Bill. He pointed at the bridge, explaining to everyone how the old railway was constructed, and about the people who built it. He said volunteers did the work. He was somewhat right, but Bill knew Chinese had been hired to do the work, and volunteered to do the dangerous jobs for little pay and a lot of hardship. Most of the graves in the area stood covered in moss and unmarked, for who would miss a yellow man who died in the north? Bill did not correct him, preferring to let the manager show his ignorance.

The Deuce rocked as they came off the tracks and onto a dirt road. Soon it became a clearing, and the heavy truck stopped.

"Everyone out!" yelled the director. "Time to team up and get to your home bases."

Pete jumped off first and Bill followed. He stumbled a little when the manager didn't move but stood where he landed, making others scramble not to hit him.

Bill stepped to the side and waited, letting people pass him. They formed a line behind the director and walked like ducklings down a path. Once the last one passed, Bill also joined the line, but let himself fall back. Soon he was ten feet from the closest person, and a quick side step put him into the forest, away from everyone else.

He made up time, knowing it was precious for his plans. His current need to get to the spot and finish his setup pushed at the back of his mind. He tore off the vest and flung the bright orange dot into the air behind him.

The leaves rustled again to the left of the blind. Definitely a flash or orange colouring the green underbrush.

He slid the bolt, knowing it picked up one of the armour piercing bullets the clerk had sold him. The man mentioned something about bears wearing body armour, but advised in order to stop one of those big creatures he needed power behind the shot. And these bullets packed that power.

An orange dot crept through the canopy of leaves. He wiped at the scope, cleaning the aperture.

One eye down. The other one closed. He remembered the days of practice to make the action second nature. Centre mass. Orange dot centre mass. Aim a little high and to the right if they walked forward; high and to the left if away. One breath: in through the mouth, hold, release through the nose. Steady. Don't pull the trigger, squeeze.

The first shot will alert the others, bring some of them close. A second shot would be careless, telling them not to come. It had to be one.

Make it appear like a hunting accident. Pick them off one at a time.

He hoped it was Pete coming through the woods.

Squeeze.

The rifle kicked.

Birds erupted from their nests, chirping their anger at the noise.

Pete stumbled backward.

A red spot spread on his chest.

His eyes glazed over.

He fell to the ground.

Bill got one.

Jumping Life

I stand in the ship's control room, staring at the holographic image before me. Missiles lance across the horizon of the planet. The last of the hibernation gel drips from my nose and hits the smooth white floor at my feet. I shake the reality of our creation out of my still foggy head.

Two control panels display a countdown to the world's destruction on their black surface, a stark contrast to the white of the walls and ceiling. There is no worry about the missiles, they hardly break atmosphere, and we are geo-locked at just over 36,000 kilometres. A flash on one of the continents. One mushroom cloud grows. White, black, red. Then another. Death and destruction is all I see below us. Continents split. Green turns dark, black, then roils into red. Finally, death rolls over the world, turning it into a planet of cinder. How did it get to be this way? Why did the ship allow it to go unnoticed? At least Eve is not awake to see the destruction.

"Father, how long have I been out?" My voice grates with the plea. I take a breath and cough. Phlegm rattles from my throat still sore from hibernation, but I need to know. "Father?"

The ship, Father, answers calmly, "You have hibernated for two thousand, fifty-four years, thirty eight days, four hours and thirty three minutes standard the planet."

At least he didn't give me the seconds. "Was there any notification of this incident prior to it happening?"

The answer, though almost immediate, shows Father spends a great deal of his computational power sifting through records. "No. The build-up of nuclear weapons is worked into the parameters and represented as a 0.007452488% annihilation possibility. All within acceptable risks. Do you want to see the calculations?"

"No." It would take hours, if not days, to go over all the calculations. Besides, it's not my job. I only run the ship, keep her space worthy, and help "supply" the planets we find. This is the fifth such planet, and the fifth to destroy itself like this. We have failed again. I rub my forehead, trying to overcome the depression. "Have you started the resuscitation on Eve yet?"

"I have not. As per your last instructions on planet four, I am leaving her in hibernation until you direct me to do otherwise."

"Good." I don't know why I respond to the ship. Something about the way he says things, makes my skin crawl. And after so many years and planets, it shouldn't affect me like it does. There's something to be said about a computer that runs a ship like ours and can calculate the whole of the universe in a few minutes. He's discovered another planet for us to start number six on. "Maybe we should wake her."

"Your direct instructions on this matter are needed." Father's demand for direct orders irritates me at the best of times, and this is one of them. "I am standing by."

"Father, wake Eve."

I stare at Eve as the hibernation gel drips off her body. Long golden hair falls onto her slender shoulders in a wet, tangled mess. I doubt she's the young age of thirty that she looks. Sharp light blue eyes don't even look toward me. At one time, we towelled ourselves clean, stealing glances when the other was not looking, but not anymore. Familiarity breeds contempt.

Father always wakes me first. My orders. Neither of us knows what mood Eve will be in when she wakes. Maybe there's a balance issue in her chamber, but she refuses to let me look at it, saying the thing works well.

"Any reason why you didn't wake me earlier?" Her tone is harsh, but softening as the last of the gel slides from her shapely body to land at her feet. "We could have done something to stop it from happening."

"You know the rules. We're only to help guide them for a short time and then wait."

She glides across the deck and stares at the view screen. The planet glows like a red ball with streaks of black throughout—a molten rock floating in space. Her brow furrows, lips moving as she examines the readouts. After a billion years of running our experiment, I hoped a bond would develop between us, and we'd be able to read each other's emotions; but alas, most of the time, we hibernate. Only awaken when needed. To us, only four years have passed in wakefulness, making me just under sixty-five of our years old.

I've never asked Eve her age, but something tells me it's easily half of mine.

We've given up so much for this "experiment". Friends, family, children, the hope for normality. Striving to create life on other planets. Playing God. But if we succeed, the rewards will be staggering. It's a cost both of us have accepted. Being immortalized in the universe does have its appeal, even for the most withdrawn of our society. And what of that society? How have we, as a people, evolved beyond what Eve and I represent as a species? I will need to ask Father that question, but later, when Eve is not around.

Wetness glistens off Eve's cheeks. She's trying to hide it, wiping every time a tear falls. I reach out and put a hand on her shoulder, but she shrugs it off.

"Why?" Her voice is soft, full of pain.

"Who knows?" The comment blurts out before I can filter it.

"Are you trying to be funny or something?"

I'm almost shocked by her look, but we don't spend a lot of time talking to each other. She's always in the lab, while I search for equipment and systems to fix. "No, just reacting to your question." I take a step forward. "Such a waste of resources."

"Is that all you care about?" Her voice cracks against my back like a whip.

"Of cours–"

"Don't." She holds up a hand and curses. "Father, I just want to continue to the next target planet."

"Protocol dictates that the planet will need to be studied for at least one week before jumping to the next target system." Father is nothing but dutiful in reminding us of protocol.

Eve turns away from the screen, hunches her shoulders, and stomps off the bridge muttering, "Fine."

There is no one else on the ship, and nothing for me to do for the week it takes to follow "protocol," so I jog on Deck Four. Stem to stern, Father is 2 km's long. I instruct him to raise the deck's gravity to make the run more exhausting. And Hydroponics is there. I need to look into it.

Hydroponics is an overgrown jungle, kept at bay by the ever-present robots nurturing each and every plant to give up seeds. The two decks above are for breeding animals to transplant life on our target planet. Animal care is the same; that is when they're not in stasis. It would be cruel to keep them alive all these years breeding and destroying the ship. No, we only break them out when a new planet is started. Then they are bred and raised for infusion into the biosphere. Nice, neat, instant wildlife.

I go through everything we need for when the jump happens. Every step I've been instructed to do, even what to do if we find life already on a planet. Sanitize and prepare for our implantation of the desired form. But that is only if the spinning ball of dirt meets our needs. It must have the right atmosphere, gravity, composition.

Father has yet to pick a planet with life on it, but we have dropped off terra forming plants on over a dozen. Maybe we'll restart on one of them. They should be ready for us by now.

"Father, whatever happened to those planets we dropped terra plants on?"

Father answers immediately, "We have dropped off seventeen terra plants to date. Ten have developed suitable atmospheres, but sentient life spontaneously evolved, making them unsuitable for a return jump. Three malfunctioned, causing an extinction level event; four are still attempting to convert the atmosphere of the designated planet due to unforeseen complications in the biosphere."

Complications? "Why have there been complications?"

"Unknown. Each plant sent their update either prior to failure, shutting down on completion or have been updating my system constantly. Plant designated 44re43ii3 reported an atmospheric disruption over one million years ago, possibly due to a comet or interstellar phenomenon. No data at this time has been reported. Plant 46sw82d3t reported—"

"Enough, sorry I asked." I stop the run, glance about, stairs are to my right. I've not been on the deck below Hydroponics since planet one. It's medical, and we really don't need to have it on this ship since we don't get sick in our sterile environment. Still, curiosity is a dangerous thing to ignore. I take the stairs down.

Everything in the ship is clean. No dust, dirt, contamination, or even insects.

I walk toward a light down the corridor. Usually, Father keeps them off unless we're in the area, so it bothers me that something is lit. Could

14

there be a malfunction somewhere? No, it was built to last longer than the mission-possibility of ten billion years. The structure, a hardened neutronium alloy, is stronger than anything against the ravishes of space and time. Even Father can store more information than is currently known in our universe. He has the whole of our galaxy carried in one holographic memory core, and they put three of them on the ship. Something else must be happening.

"Father, why are the lights on down here?" I point, knowing the ship can see my intent.

"You should not be down here," Father replies. "This section is off limits to male team members prior to system jump. Please return to deck four immediately."

I ignore the request and keep walking toward the light. "Father, what system is running down here? My clearance allows me to know everything about your systems and construction. There's nothing about you that I don't know."

"Restriction protocol initiated. Please return to deck four."

It doesn't make sense. I have full access, and nothing should stand in my way. A slight hissing sounds, and the air becomes thin. "Father, what is happening?"

"Restriction protocol is initiated. Atmosphere is reduced by twenty-five percent. Please return to deck four. Further disobedience will result in atmosphere reduction by another ten percent."

Disobedience? What does Father mean by that?

I gasp for breath. Darkness fills in from the edge of my vision. A slight smell of burning toast flits in the air, and something inside me clicks. If I don't escape this deck, I'll die.

I force one foot in front of the other, struggling toward the stairs. A door to my right opens, and Father's voice echoes from it. "Enter the lift for safety."

My knees scream as if someone kicks them, and I reach forward, touching the floor. I pull myself into the small room, and the door closes. Slowly, the pressure increases, and the lift propels itself up one level. A delay lasts for an eternity before the door opens again.

A light blinds me as the ceiling comes into focus. I try to sit up, only to have a firm hand press against my chest.

"What the hell were you doing on deck five before a jump?" Eve flicks off the light, her brows furrow together.

Lavender floats in the air, and my slight headache lessens.

"That was stupid." She taps the console beside the bed I'm lying on. "Well, at least nothing is damaged. Brain is still running at twenty percent capacity. Not bad for a man." She stands, grabs my clothes off the table, and throws them at me. "Next time, remember the protocol. Deck Five is off limits before a jump. You've put us behind schedule."

Really? Something like this is on a schedule? After a billion-year run the schedule is somewhat of a moving target. I swing tired legs over the side of the bed and sit up. "What happens on Deck Five?"

She spins and yells, "We're on Deck Five! The whole jump time is delayed another three days. You don't know what you're doing. Get dressed, and go back to the bridge."

Tears well in her eyes as she yells at me, but I cannot imagine what it's all about. My clothes are on the floor, so I reach down and pick them up, putting on my pants and shirt, then shoes. She still demands I hurry before the window is gone and we have to stay another month over this accursed planet. There's nothing I can say, even if I could get a word in between her screaming and sobbing. Still, I want to know what happens on Deck Five before a jump.

My jump chair cradles me with warmth. I love every time I sit in her. Unfortunately, Father retracts her after each jump to initiate repairs in case we need to jump soon after arriving at a new planet. I wait, envisioning the ship's wings extending out to catch the exotic hadrons needed to form the rift in space. Such will allow us to travel the 50,000 odd light years to our new planet.

Eve sits in her chair beside me. I don't see any anger in her now, just furrowed brows and a frown of confused loss as she stares out into space through the front view port.

I'd lowered the barrier to allow us to look at the stars during the jump. It's breathtaking to see and somewhat lessens the feeling of one's stomach being ripped through your back.

The readouts flair as Father catches a skyrmion, and the jump can happen now; the emitters have the necessary exotic matter in place.

The tear opens. At first, it looks like a jagged white horizontal line. Then, without any other outward sign, it splits to reveal a maw. The stars blur, become muddy, out of focus. The mighty engines of Father ignite and throw particles out from behind, pushing us into our chairs. Gravity reaches four times normal, and then stops. Our forward motion is enough to carry us through the rip. As we pass through the event horizon, my stomach gurgles, threatening to expel its contents. My eyes spread a little further apart, making things go out of focus, and for a split second, I swear I can see God. Then it ends. The stars are sharp, crisp, and part of a blue planet takes up the lower portion of the screen.

"Jump completed," Father says.

"Another planet." Eve sighs, slips out of her chair, and walks to the back of the bridge. "I'll start the scans. Can you put us into orbit, Father?"

The ship can run the mission. I don't have to be here. Eve gives Father tasks to do while I sit here and admire the spinning sphere we approach. The world is blue, with just the right land mass for the project. I sigh with relief.

"This could be the one." I get up from the chair.

"Maybe ..." Eve glances to the screen, then looks back to the console. "Scans show life, but not something we need to worry about. Cold blooded creatures mostly."

"The star's right, the planet looks good. Is the gravity normal?" I only ask because reptiles grow large on light gravity planets.

"No, gravity is one standard." Eve turns to the view port. "It's perfect."

We spend one week going over scans and read outs. A timeline spreads out before us, showing what is needed to start the project on this planet.

"The oxygen content of the oceans at this point must be reduced." Eve places a finger on the display. "This will create the anoxic event to produce rich sediments on the ocean floor." She follows along the line a few more years. "At this point here, the reptilian life will start to die off, giving the planet a good resource for the new inhabitants. We'll hibernation for one hundred million years so Father can extend forces to split the supercontinent and create tectonic plates in the desired form. The life on the planet should be ended at that time, and the seeding can begin."

I scratch the back of my head. Another hundred million years. What will life look like to our fellow beings at that time? What has become of our civilization? "Has our system been updated by control yet?"

Father answers my question. "I have received five updates since the start of the mission. Memory cube one is full, while cube two is now at seventy-five percent capacity."

Stunned silence falls between Eve and me. We have received more data than initially decided upon, but Father never mentioned it. "Father, why didn't you inform us of this before?"

"Protocol dictates that only Eve be informed of each data dump."

I glare at Eve.

"You didn't need to know," she says, turning back to her console. "We have a mission, and that is all I have to say."

The world spins. "But that's *not* all. I want to know what took so much of Father's memory to store. What's so important in there? Something that control wants us to know? Spit it out, Eve. What aren't you telling me?"

"Nothing." Eve taps a few commands into the console. "It's time to hibernate. The auto system will take care of the rest."

I don't get the answer, but swear I will upon waking. Eve closes the lid of my chamber, and the fog sends ants crawling along my skin before sleep takes me. The smile on Eve's face is all I see before drifting off.

A heartbeat later, the gel drains away and the hatch lifts. My head spins as I sit up, and bile rises from my empty stomach. Sick splatters the floor. This is the first time hibernation makes me sick.

I get up, wipe the slimy gel off my body so it pools in globs on the deck, and proceed to the bridge. Something seems off, and I cannot pinpoint it for the life of me. Father is warm, much warmer than he usually is when I exit hibernation.

The lift doors part to a brilliance I've never seen before. The view port is open, allowing for an expanse of light from the system's star. A star far too large. A star in its death throws. A star gone mad. Eve is sitting in her jump chair, tears rolling down her face.

"Father," I say. "Status report."

A pause. Too long of a pause. "We are currently orbiting the planet at 36,433 kilometres. Initial scans show all life on the planet has ceased. A stellar incident is occurring, causing the star to destabilize."

"We're trapped!" Eve cries out.

"Trapped?" The word does not register. "We can jump to another system."

"No, we can't." Eve drops her head, shoulders slumping. A tear lands at her feet. "All these years of planning, lost."

"We can jump!" I take my jump chair and try to reassure her. "Father can take us out of here in a few seconds. All we need to do is trap another skyrmion and open a rift."

"You don't understand." Eve stands up from her seat and drifts toward the viewport. "It's not that simple."

"Damn, Eve, how hard can it be?" I stand, growing worried at the approaching star mass.

"I'm not ovulating yet." She sinks to her knees before the view port, light reflecting off her hair still wet from the hibernation gel.

"I don't understand."

"Exotic matter cannot be trapped without a central point of life to guide it. That central point can only be from something that gives intelligence to the universe." Her lower lip trembles. "One egg. One Jump."

I still don't understand.

Eve continues, "Before each hibernation period, Father harvests your sperm and stores it for the next jump. Then, when I start to ovulate, he fertilizes my egg for the next jump. The protocol is keeping you off deck five." She takes my hand. "That is why you are here. Not to keep the ship in good repair, but to keep us able to jump." She pulls me in close, arms warping around my chest. A warmth transfers between us from our first real intimate contact. "There is always a sacrifice for each leap in science that we make. This one was the most controversial and secret. We are seeding not to extend our life, but to fuel a fleet of ships with the lives of others. But they must be ready. And that is why we needed to make sure they could survive until they discovered space travel. That was the breaking point of the experiment."

I still don't get it.

"We were creating a slave race to fuel our ships. Don't you get it? All this time, I kept you in the dark. Update after update flowed in, but nothing told to you." She collapses into a heap on the floor, sliding out of my now limp arms. "We are not seeding the galaxy for ourselves, Adam, but for the betterment of a race no longer human."

All I can think of is the deaths of my children to allow us to jump between stars.

And then the wave-front of the supernova hits Father, the only thing hot enough to melt his outer hull. It strips away, throwing us against the bulkhead, and a tear in Eve's eye evaporates as our bodies burn.

Snow in April

April, 2023

Jess stared down the line of people carrying jerry cans. They all held their coats tight against the harsh, blowing snow, fuel chits hidden somewhere on their person. This April promised to be the same as the last, blistering cold and a foot of snow in the hamlet in southern Ontario. She shuffled closer to the truck, hoping against hope there'd be enough to fill her 20-litre jug.

She remembered a time when April brought forth rain as a prelude to spring. Not so anymore. The change happened rapidly, and only those who had prepared survived, the ones people laughed at, mocked, scoffed, and called doomsayers. Those mockers no longer joked—if they survived at all.

"Next!" A man, bundled in heavy clothes, waved the line forward.

Her neighbour, William, pushed grey hair away from his wrinkled eyes, shuffled away from the truck while muttering under his breath. "Dirty oil. That's all they have."

Jess worried about that. If the oil was too dirty, it would clog the lines. She didn't know how to fix the fuel injector on the furnace, and her husband still coughed from the "bad flu". Last night, he hacked so hard, his hand came away from his mouth covered in blood. Luckily, William recognized he might have injured his windpipe, and kindly gave them cough suppressants to alleviate the pain. She never asked where he got them.

"Where's your chit?" A man wearing a reserves uniform held out his hand expectantly.

"Here." Jess dropped a small, plastic coin-shape into his grubby hand.

"Twenty, right?"

The man frowned. "Last week." The chit disappeared into his coat. "This week that'll get you eighteen."

She wanted to argue, to take back the chit and find another fuel truck. But there was no other. This was the first one since last week, and she didn't have the fuel to start the truck to find another. Jess held out her can.

"Remove the top."

Jess unscrewed the top and placed the empty container on the ground. He shoved the nozzle into it and squeezed the trigger. A dark sludge poured out. Numbers counted up on a small display mounted on the dispenser. It clicked off at 17.9 litres. She glared at the man who only smiled back. "Price for not being ready," he said and pulled out the nozzle.

What can I do?

The world changed in 2019. The last of the bees died, frogs disappeared, and winter ran from September to May. Crops froze, and the world all but ceased to live as well. The change happened so fast that none understood what transpired. Theories, yes, but nothing proven.

"Move along," the man grumbled.

Jess screwed the top back on and picked up her can with a grunt. The weight pulled at her arm as she shuffled cold feet back the way she came.

Winter in April.

Jess placed the container on the floor next to their furnace. Mark, her husband, sat on a small chair, shivering with fever. He glanced up. The corners of his mouth lifted slightly and twitched, then a bout of wet coughs shook his body.

"You should be in bed," Jess said. She twisted the cap off the jerry can, then attached a feeder line.

"No," Mark wheezed. "You may need help."

"I've done this many times." She turned the crank on the side of the furnace, enticing the dark sludge to feed into the holding tank. "Besides, that flu isn't going to cure itself if you push your body too much."

He coughed again, and his words came out with more rasp, "We need the heat. Keeping the house at fifteen degrees won't get the vegetables growing."

Jess finished pumping. "You're right, but we need this to last."

"I was thinking"–Mark strained to keep back a cough–"next clear day, I can angle the solar panels a little, get some more light."

Jess pulled out the feeder tube. "Not if you're not well." The last few drops needed to be fed into the furnace by direct draining, something she hated doing. But this was their world, and she needed to do it for them to survive. You better not die on me. "Are you feeling better than yesterday?"

Mark coughed again. "Hell yes, just about ready to go to work."

Her laughter was not as infectious as a few years ago when everyone said this weather would pass. "I'm sure the bank would be happy to have you back. Their systems just need to be rebooted or something, then the trading will commence."

Mark chuckled, but the coughing returned. "I'm sure the Dow will recover."

Five years. We've been together five years and he still tries to make me smile. Jess watched the last drop of oil leave the jerry can. "And the dollar will make a rally and be worth something."

His body shook with coughing while he laughed. He kept his fist curled, but a small smudge of blood showed around his thumb and forefinger. "We need to get you back in bed."

"You vixen, I'll not have you take advantage of me in this weakened state." Mark struggled to stand, putting an arm around Jess's shoulders as she took some of his weight. Together they walked up the stairs.

Jess waited at the foot of the bed as William examined Mark. The old man, a surgeon in another life, could still help when needed. His liver-spotted hand moved with firm and sure movement. She couldn't imagine helping Mark without him.

The old man sat back on the bed. Mark slept, his breath rattling. William held Mark's wrist, made a humph noise, and glanced at his watch. "Have you given him all the cough suppressors?"

"Yes, one in the morning and one at night, just like you said." Wetness ran down her cheek. "Is he going to be all right?"

William set Mark's hand down and stood. "Can we talk somewhere else?"

Jess nodded and led the old man out of the bedroom, down the stairs and into the kitchen. The scent of bread baking filled the room. She hurried to the oven, checked, and pulled out three loaves, one slightly browner on the top than the others.

"What are your plans?" William eyed the bread.

Jess dumped the loaves out of the tins and set them to cool. Her lower lip trembled. Soon, tears flowed down her face, and William came over, placing an arm over her shoulder. "I– I– I don't know what to do."

William patted her back.

"Is Mark going to die?" Jess pulled away from the man, staring down into his face.

Sadness in his eyes greeted her gaze. She could sense his thoughts. He's going to die, and William doesn't know how to tell me.

William looked away. "Nothing is certain." He stepped back, taking her hands in his. "His body is still fighting, and that's a good thing. But there should have been more effect from the pills. Is he getting enough to drink?"

"I melt snow every day for him." Jess held onto his hands. "He drinks at least ten cups a day."

"What about food?"

Jess's laugh almost reached hysteria. "Food? Who has enough food?" She motioned to the bread. "I have this, but flour is running low. We have a little meat still frozen from his deer hunt a few months ago. Thank God for that." She wiped at her tears. "We have veggies from our garden–" She put a hand over her mouth. Shit, I just told someone we have a garden!

The corner of William's mouth lifted. "We all have a garden." He patted her hand. "Mark helped a lot of people build solar panels and hook up grow lights. That's why none of us have scurvy."

He helped people set up gardens? He only told me about the solar panels. Jess glanced at the floor. "I didn't know."

"A lot of us are in his debt." William dropped her hand. "That's why I didn't charge you for the pills."

"I thought you were just being a good neighbour."

William chuckled. "Yes, I was. But if it had been anyone but Mark, I still would have asked for something in return." He stepped back to the kitchen table, motioning Jess to join him. She took the opposite seat. "But my main concern now is the effect the coughing is having on his throat." He leaned over and picked up his black bag. "The pills should have cleared up the cough and helped with any injury." His hand fumbled inside the bag, came out with a pill bottle. "Here." He offered another bottle of pills. Amoxicillin. "He's developed strep from all the coughing, something new from last visit. These should clear it up."

Jess took the pills in both hands.

"We'll be closer to square with him after this, so don't worry."

Jess nodded.

"I'm going home. Beth worries when I'm away for too long."

Jess stood. *I should give him something.* She went to the counter and wrapped up a loaf of bread. "Take this to Beth, will you? I haven't seen her in a while, and I hope she's okay."

"You don't have to–"

"William Edward Starky, when someone offers you something, take it. You've been here countless times and helped with Mark's sickness. I won't send you back with nothing for your trouble."

William blushed. "Years ago the government paid me to do what I just did."

"Well, that government went bankrupt with that hag Wynne." Jess remembered the year the people hunted down the spend thrift leader and hung her. "Now we have to take care of ourselves."

William nodded, took the bread, and bid a farewell.

Jess closed the bedroom door and wiped at the tears. She didn't want to think about a future without Mark, but it kept making its way into her mind. *William wanted to know if I had a plan? What does he know that I don't?* She couldn't bring herself to figure out what to do if Mark died. They married just before the fall of civilization when he worked for a major corporation, and they purchased the home in a rural community. The world changed when the snow came and everything went dark, the major cities fell into chaos. The banks collapsed. Computers stopped working. Life struggled to continue.

Mark believed in being self-sufficient. He hunted, butchered the animals himself, and insisted she learn as well. Though not as good a shot as her husband, Jess could hit the bullseye most of the time. She really didn't like skinning the kills. Learning to bake took no time. Jess enjoyed the creation of food. Once she mastered the skill, she found it took less time to create a meal than preparing packaged foods.

When they bought their home, it used an old oil furnace. They planned to change to self-sufficiency with a geothermal heating system, before everything fell apart. But at least the solar cells and battery wall were installed. They were better off than most, and Mark's hunting supplied meat while her basement hydroponics kept plants alive during the forever winter gripping the planet. They would survive, and in some comfort.

Mark rolled over, coughing a little. Blood coloured the pillow.

May 2023

A heavy beating on the door woke Jess from her troubled sleep. She'd dreamed of Mark and their wedding day. The banging amplified.

"I'm coming!" she called out, putting on a robe.

She looked over to Mark's side of the bed, empty now for a month. Complications from the flu, strep throat, and pneumonia finally took him away from her. William helped dispose of the body and comforted her at the loss. She first wanted to bury him, but the ground sported a foot of snow, the surface frozen. Her growing belly kept her from digging a grave. At least Mark had the chance to see the start of their child before he died.

With her robe tied around, slippers on feet, she proceeded downstairs. The banging became urgent.

"I said I'm coming!" She grabbed the shotgun before turning the corner at the landing.

The breezeway between the outside and home sported a metal door. Something she put up right after Mark passed away. He'd made her promise to do it. Something he wanted to install, but fell ill before he could. It would keep almost anyone out. A twist of the lock opened the first door, and a few steps took her to the metal one. She slid a small peek hole aside. "Who is it?"

Dark eyes stared back at her, framed by dark skin and a beard. An official looking cap, though worn and beaten with age, poked out of a hood opening. The man stood at least two metres tall with a frown on his face, icy wind ruffling his beard. He probably wanted to come in, but Jess did not want any strangers inside, regardless of who they were.

"Captain Amed, of the Watch, Ma'am. May we come in?"

Jess shook her head. "No." She held the shotgun up and chambered a round.

Captain Amed's eyebrow arched. "We are on official business." He held up his ID with badge. "The government wants to conduct a census of those living out here in order to make sure all the resources are accounted for."

They want to see how many people live in the house, that way they can lower my fuel allotment. Jess stared out the slot. "Nothing's changed."

"We have orders to verify each—"

Jess stared into the man's eyes. "Let me see the orders."

The man scowled, opened his coat, and reached in with a gloved hand, letting out heat in the process. Jess smiled. She didn't like this man. He was pushy, demanding, rude by banging on the door in a self-important way to rush her. She glanced at the clock. 7 am. Well, I should be up anyway.

"Here are the orders." The man held the papers before the slit.

"I'll need to see them. Slip them through the hole."

"You can read them from there."

"You can slip them through the hole or keep talking to the door. Either way, the only chance of you getting into our home is if it says so on the paper."

The man swore.

I caught him. He probably just wanted to get inside to look around for looting.

"I can't give you this one, it's my only copy."

"Then you're not coming in. There are two of us. You can record that and leave."

A hushed voice sounded behind the man who nodded before asking, "How many people are in the home, ma'am?"

"Two … soon to be three in a few months," she added, hoping it may increase her rations.

"Who are the people?"

"Mark and Jess Harper. We haven't named our child yet."

"Thank you, I'll report this. There may be a follow-up visit to verify names and people."

Jess nodded. "Make sure they bring the right paperwork."

The man tipped his hat, put the paperwork away, and turned. Jess shut the slot, shivered, and went back inside.

August 2023

Jess watched snow fall outside while kneading dough, pushing it into the countertop as best as she could. William would be here soon.

The doctor made an effort to come over every three days to check on her progress. She didn't mind. It gave the older man something to do besides sit at home. His wife, Beth, passed away getting fuel for their furnace during an ice storm in June. She worried about the man being all alone. Today she would ask him to move in, hoping his pride would not get in the way of survival.

She finished kneading and separated the dough into loafs for rising. I hope it's warm enough in the house.

Jess never made it to the last fuel drop. For some reason, she just couldn't get herself out of bed, let alone walk through the snow storm that cold bitter summer. She did make bathroom breaks, looking out at the snow-covered landscape when passing a window. Her heart still felt empty, just like the left side of the bed.

A sharp pain raced across her abdomen, causing her to double over. It had happened before, but she attributed it to the baby shifting, readying himself for delivery. Not yet, still a couple of weeks away. She walked to the living room and sat on Mark's favourite chair. The large wingback wrapped around her, but it no longer held his scent. With one hand, she caressed the worn arm and wondered if it would survive.

Wetness crept down the inside of her thighs; she stood quickly, sending a spasm of pain through her belly. No, not now! There's no one here. The pain turned into a burning.

"Not ... yet ..." she gasped.

The pain throbbed, and she dropped to her knees. A small spurt of water pushed itself from between her legs. Jess hunched her body, bearing down. Time passed. She pushed. Thoughts of a breach birth entered her mind. Sweat beaded on her forehead. She whimpered, grunted, screamed. At some point, William must have entered. He guided her onto the floor. Coached her. Helped her. Then the wailing of small lungs filled the air.

"A boy. Little underweight, but strong." William laid the child on her chest. "Some children take to the breast right away, while others wait." He stood on shaking legs. "Do you have towels in the kitchen?"

"Yes," Jess gasped. Her breath slowed.

"We'll let the cord stay attached until it stops pulsing." His voice grew distant. "Then we can cut and clean." His voice grew louder, and the rough texture of a towel brushed between her legs. "He's strong. Fastest delivery I ever saw."

Jess barked out a quick laugh, but her insides screamed. "You were a surgeon, how many births did you see?"

William chuckled. "More than you think. I spent a whole year as an OBGYN assistant in med school. Can you hold the glass?" He lifted her head, put a glass in her hand, and watched as she took a swallow of cool water. "Do you know what you're going to call him?"

She looked at her son. One small hand encompassed her little finger. "Mark," she finally said.

William nodded.

October 2023

Jess bent low to examine the snow before her. Small paw prints covered the area, but only one set interested her in the forest. The prints of a jack rabbit. She stood, taking in the cold morning air, letting it fill her lungs. One hand opened her heavy coat to allow her to look down at Mark, nestled comfortably in his carrier at her breast. He curled up at the cold October air. She closed her coat.

"Don't worry, soon you'll be out here playing hunter." She caressed the little bundle and followed the trail into the brush.

She crossed the train tracks without seeing anyone. This time of year reminded her of renewal, and the days she spent at her meditation camps before the everlasting snow. It seemed like a lifetime ago.

Jess stopped. Her gaze landed on the jack, sitting in the snow just ten metres from her. Using slow movements, she unslung her .17 cal and sighted down the barrel, hating what needed to be done, but the animal's death would put food on the table. Breathe through the mouth, hold, then out through the nose. Slow, easy breaths. When you're ready, squeeze the trigger on the exhale.

A sharp report echoed in the air before Jess could squeeze the trigger. The jack jumped and bolted for the bushes.

Jess's eyes widened as she glanced about. No blood smear on the snow, the Jack still lived. She searched for a second before darting into the underbrush.

Three men came into view, running in the forest. One of them the man who banged on her door so many months ago.

"I hit 'em, I say!" said the captain's companion. The man carried a rifle too powerful for shooting small game. "He's around here somewhere."

The captain came up behind the shooter, placed a hand on a shoulder only to have it shrugged off. "Now, Don, that's not the right kind of attitude to take with a superior."

"Sorry, Captain. I swore I hit the beast."

"Well, if you did, all we would see is blood and meat scattered all over the place. A .30 .30 is not a good weapon for hunting rabbit. Bear, yes. Rabbit, no." The tall man turned and started to walk back the way he came. "Let's get back to camp. The fuel truck will be here in a couple of hours, and we need to take care of it."

Don stayed put, staring out into the bush while the other two walked away. He lifted his rifle and fired into the underbrush with frustration. "Fucking rabbit!"

"Don! Time to return to camp. Double time!"

He slung the rifle over his shoulder, turned, and ran after the officer.

Jess waited. She didn't want to run into the group for any reason, let alone the hot-head, Don, with his .30 .30. Her breath rattled, hand tightening on the riffle grip, arm covering a lump slung across her chest.

After ten minutes, Jess pulled herself from the safety of the brush. She opened her coat to see Mark still sleeping. The kid could sleep through anything.

Not wanting to miss out on a possible meal, Jess trudged through the snow as quietly as possible toward the spot where she'd seen the jack rabbit hide. Movement caught her eye, and she stopped. The rabbit, easily weighing over 3 kg's, jumped out and halted on the tracks.

"We may be eating after all." Jess unslung, aimed, whispered a silent prayer for the life she was about to take, and fired.

December 2023

Jess woke, yawned, stretched out an arm for Mark, but she only touched a pillow. It took a few seconds, then her heart sank. He died. She buried her face in shaking hands and cried.

Get it together, Jess. Your son needs you. Slowly she let go of the grief and buried it in that secret place beside her heart. Leaving the bed was the first step to move on every morning. She forced her legs over the side of the bed, reached out, pushed the curtains aside, then climbed out of bed. Jess shivered from the cold air. She grabbed her robe, wrapped it around her body, and looked over to Mark's crib, a gift from William's wife, Beth. He was not there.

Where the hell is my son? Her breath rushed in and out, hands trembling enough to cause the crib to rattle.

Jess ran out of her room, bumped into a small side table, feet taking her down the stairs and into the kitchen. She stopped, hand against her chest. Her breath slowed as she saw William sitting at the table, tea in one hand and Mark supported in the other. The child smiled at the man, entertained by his antics of touching tongue to nose. Mark giggled and squealed. Jess flushed.

The heavy weight on Jess's heart lifted. She leaned on a chair, letting the thudding in her chest lessen. He's okay. William has him.

Two months ago, Jess talked William into staying with them. His turning point, knowing Don trained for the militia. The old man made a show of not wanting to leave his home, but Jess pushed the idea of company to help pass the days and a joining of their resources.

"Did we wake you?" William asked.

"No, not at all. Just woke up from a bad dream and didn't see my little monkey." Jess held out her arms and William, with much protesting from Mark, handed over her child.

"I changed him." William waved a hand under his nose. "I swear the kid saves everything up for when I do it. Fed him too, so don't worry about much." He stood, strode into the kitchen, and poured a cut of tea. "Sorry, no sugar today."

Jess took the offered cup. "That's okay; I need to cut down on it anyway."

William chuckled. "The MacDonald's from across the way"—he waved his hand in a Southerly direction—"have asked for me to help deliver one of their grandchildren. Seems the kids are hanging around the militia."

Jess made a face. "Government has no business putting child molesting troops near law abiding citizens."

William nodded. "The girl is seventeen, so I guess they thought she was fair game." He walked back to the chair. "They offered to pay in pheasant, so we'll be eating well tonight."

"William?" Jess bit her lower lip, and put Mark down on the floor.

"Yes?"

Just blurt it out. "William, why are we doing this?"

William shrugged. "Doing what?"

"The world is all screwed up." Jess sat at the table and crossed her arms on the hard surface. "We fucked ourselves as a race, and now people are taking what they want instead of working together." She took a deep breath, lips trembling. "Will we survive, or die of the cold? What life does Mark have in this frozen world?"

31

The old man sat back down at the table with her. "There is hope." He reached out and took her hand. "Life always finds a way. Just look at the animals still with us. There are deer, rabbits, pheasants, and, I've been told by people, fish!" He stared into space just beyond her. "How I would love a fresh trout."

"Wouldn't we all," Jess snorted. She couldn't remember the taste of poached salmon with lemon anymore. "But what type of a life will Mark have?" She brushed away at the start of a tear. "Will he grow up only knowing the cold? How will he survive? Will he marry? Have children of his own? Be happy?"

William focused back on Jess, his old eyes turning down at the corners. "Who can tell?" He leaned back in the chair, making it creek. "Many people survived much worse. Think of how people lived years ago. Even the Nordic people, Inuit, and Khanty of Northern Siberia. They not only lived in such weather, but flourished. Who knows how God will look after us?"

Jess let out a humph. "Why would God let this happen?"

"He lets us make our own way through life." William smiled a gentle smile. "It is not up to us to say why he lets things happen. God said he would not interfere with mankind after the Great Flood." He reached into his breast pocket, extracting a small, thick book with a cross stamped on it in gold. The cover held deep creases and several dull spots where the leather was worn thin. "You should read this." He pressed it into her hands. "It was given to me by my sponsor years ago."

"Sponsor?"

William smiled. "Yes, sponsor. Forty-six years sober this year. I don't know if the writings will help you. Everyone suffers a loss of faith at one time in their life. Mine happened in my thirties. Beth almost left me." His eyes took on that far-away look. "I really do miss her."

Jess took the bible, thumbed through it a little. "This must be older than forty." She turned to the first few pages. The slight yellowing of the paper showed a stark contrast against the black cover. "William, this was printed in 1912!"

"My Father-in-law sponsored me." He pointed at the bottom of the page. "See, he was given it back then, and he passed it on to me."

"He sponsored you through AA?" Jess read the inscription closely. "His message is interesting. 'God will show the way.' What does he mean by that?"

William petted her hand. "Ask me again some other time." He stood and scooped Mark off the floor before the child toppled over a chair.

April 2024

Jess wept before William's bed. The sun shone through the window, but it failed to warm the body of the old man. At eighty-four, he had lived a good life and helped many people. I'll have to get one of the neighbours to help me move him out of the bed.

Mark cried in his crib in the next bedroom, and Jess wondered how the infant knew the old man passed away. His cries started early in the morning, and when she couldn't stand it anymore, she took him from the crib. Nothing she tried quieted him. Finally, she had gone into William's room to see if he could examine her child. That was when she found him. His placid face turned slightly away from the door, showing just the peaceful features of a person asleep.

He deserved to die in his sleep, at peace. Probably dreaming of Beth.

She decided to give William some dignity. It took only a few minutes to find his favourite suit. Being careful and respectful, she removed his pajamas. She did not know why it was important, only that it was. He took such good care of his appearance. She sponge-washed his body. A cross around his neck stood out, glistening gold. Jess hesitated. She wondered about his faith, and a tinge of loneliness touched her heart. Her eyes blurred, and a tear fell onto William. She wiped it away and removed the chain and cross that encircled his neck. It took longer for her to dress him and comb his hair. When she finished, Jess took his hands and placed them on his chest, wrapping the chain around them with the cross on the back of his left hand. He would like this. Absently, she brushed tears from her cheek.

I'll get the MacDonald's, they'll help. Jess scooped up Mark and bundled up for a trip outside. The snow floated lightly to the ground, and the tree branches did not sway. With a coat wrapped around her and Mark, she strapped on the shoes and headed toward the MacDonald home. At least the snowshoes Mark bought me that Christmas before our world fell apart are of use.

June 2024

The sound of a crash outside woke Jess. She rubbed the sleep from her tired eyes, and wondered what would be waking her so early. With annoyance, she threw off the covers, donned her robe, and hurried to the southern bedroom. She peered through the window, trying desperately to see past the fingers of the oak trees outside. Black smoke crawled to the sky. It came from William's old home. Looters, probably. They might have heard about his passing and are taking advantage of it.

Light from the early morning day did little to illuminate the fresh snow, and eerie shadows reached across the ground. Movement in those shadows caught Jess's eye, and she scanned the landscape until it landed on five figures darting from William's front door.

They hurried, rifles slung across their backs. Long coats splayed open at the back by the wind of their passage. Militia. She swore under her breath. Her weapon sat in its rack at the bottom of the stairs.

Jess's stomach roiled as she watched the flames build in the home next to hers. The MacDonald's could've used that home for one of their daughters. I promised William a young couple in love would have it. She hoped the wind stayed down, least the fire caught on the trees and jumped to another home.

The MacDonald's, with three young daughters aged seventeen to nineteen, had the best chance to take over the home. Now they would have nothing. If their daughters married, they would need to find another place to live, one probably very far away from the town they grew up in. Away from family. Away from support. Away from protection.

A tear landed on the sill, spread, and became cold.

This is the world we live in.

Jess turned away from the window, leaving a small, worn, black book on the sill, gold cross facing the heavens.

December 2024

The fire burned hot behind the doors of the insert. Jess remembered the time she argued with Mark about the expense of a wood burning fireplace, but he insisted, countering that it was a renewable resource and not a waste of money. She'd relented after a few weeks. Now, it was a solid investment. The solar panels he installed so many years ago supplied enough power to keep the fan going all day and night. She could cook from the heat on the hearth, warm the house to a comfortable level. And, because it was efficient, people had to look close to see the small wisps of smoke rise from the chimney. He was a smart man, and prepared his family for what inevitably came.

A knock sounded from the front door. Not hard, but somewhat urgent. She rose from the hearth, glanced at her rifle but decided not to grab it, and went to the door. A quick look through the peep hole showed her the MacDonald family shivering in the cold. She opened the door and let them in.

Bill MacDonald, a tower of a man at well over two metres, ducked his head as he entered. Behind him followed Jean, his wife, standing just to his chest, and their mismatched three daughters. The youngest one, Mary, eyes puffy and face bruised, cried silently. Her long, strawberry blonde hair hung in strands about her face. Sharp cheek bones mimicked those of her father's and nothing like her mother's.

Off came Bill's hat. "Jess, I need your rifle."

Bill was a pacifist. He hunted, like all people did in the area, but only used snares and traps. To ask for a firearm surprised her to no end. "What?"

Bill pulled off his coat, showing a tattered shirt and rope belt holding up paled jeans with patches at the knees. "I'm gonna kill the fuck!" He kicked off his boots. "I need a rifle ta kill 'em."

Jess's eyes widened. "Kill who, Bill? What happened? Jean, what's going on?"

Mary burst out in tears.

"Shit." Bill held out his arms to his daughter. The girl recoiled, taking the protective arms of her mother instead.

"Fuckin' bastard!" Bill clenched his fists, face red. "She can't even take my comforting embrace!"

Jess held out her hands to Bill, palms up, brow furrowing. "Who?"

"That asshole Don." Bill squatted, burying palms into his eyes. "He raped Mary."

Jess talked Bill and Jean into letting Mary stay with her for a few weeks. In the end, they agreed. The influence of a stronger woman than her mother would help as well. Jess showed the young girl how to scavenge for food and where some of the hidden stores were located around town. Those special places to get a little sweet, or how to find flour in the homes along the outskirts of town that no one lived in any more. She did not show her the fishing hole, the one dug into a small but deep lake a little over 2 kms away.

Time passed, and the girl healed emotionally as well as physically.

The training Jess received before the world changed helped, and her crises management skills showed. But on the sixth week, Mary started to cry again.

Jess, not wanting to see the young girl slip into depression, tapped softly on her bedroom door, the one where William once slept.

"Mary?"

Only sobs answered.

"Mary, I'm coming in. Something is wrong and you need to tell me." Jess opened the door. Mary lay in bed, knees drawn up to her chest, forehead buried in crossed arms. "Mary, you need to talk to someone about what's bothering you. Is it Don?"

The response came instantly in a deep weeping and the girl cowered away from Jess who went over and sat on the edge of the bed.

"I'm sorry if I this causes you pain, but we need to talk about what is bothering you. That way, you can move on with your life."

Mary lifted her head, eyes red and puffy, mouth curled down in close to hysterical anguish. Her quick look tugged at Jess, telling volumes all at once.

Jess took her hands. "You can tell me anything." She squeezed the young girl's hands. "This is a safe place for you. Anything you say or do will never be told to another person."

Mary nodded.

Jess bit her lip. Gave a curt nod. Raised her eyebrows.

Mary's lower lip trembled. A sharp, shuddering breath went into her body, then escaped with just the same speed. She looked about to cry again, but then sniffled back as if to gain courage. "I– I– I'm late."

Jess watched from the brush as a car passed the side of the road. The snow crunched under her snowshoes in the crisp, cold morning air. The place she desired to go stood just over a hundred metres away. The .17 cal rested against her back, strap barely registering as it held the weapon in place. She counted the time it took for the vehicle to be out of sight. Sixty seconds was a lifetime for a person to wait.

Satisfied the car no longer posed a problem, Jess jumped up and ran as fast as she could down the open road. Once the snow obscured the side of the street, she started to climb it. A large mound of snow stood before her. She only had ten more metres to get to the pharmacy. Her promise to Mary weighted heavy in her mind. "You will not have to carry that bastard's child." She intended to keep her promise.

The mound of snow held as she climbed over it. Once at the top, she shifted, and slid down the back until she could see the lip of the roof and used it to stop. Down she went, being careful not to leave tell-tale tracks or uncovering the black roof. Once fully out of view, she pushed the loose snow from the back window of the upstairs apartment.

With the snow moved aside, Jess took off her snowshoes and slipped through the window. She found the bed with a foot and closed the window.

The light entering in the cleared window exposed the upstairs apartment. The vaulted ceiling gave plenty of room for the attic-turned-sleeping-area of the older home. A small amount of snow gathering just under the south facing window at the other side. Must be a window crack. She approached, and nodded as she saw the small fracture. A piece of glass had given away under the constant onslaught of winter. I'll brace something against it—protect the inside of my treasure.

She headed for the stairs, less light shone through the lower snow buried windows than on her last visit. Stepping off the bed, she reached into a pocket to bring out a small crank flash light. The LED lights took very little energy and the illumination could be adjusted from a full beam to a pin prick. She put it on one-quarter power.

The inside of the store held seven rows of shelves picked clean of any usable items, the shadows of Jess's prior visits over the last year. Her thoughts and gaze roamed toward the rear of the pharmacy. She pulled out a small crowbar and headed to the back.

The pull-down shield, secured in place by two padlocks, barred her entrance in the past, but today the need overpowered the desire to keep the stores safe. She inserted the bar in the loop and pried. At first, she doubted the screws would give, but leaning against the bar made them release with a satisfactory pop. Then the four screws gave way, releasing from the counter. She smiled and repeated the process on the second padlock.

Free from the counter, the barrier reluctantly slid into its roller.

Jess hopped over the counter and used her light to examine the bottles before her. RU 486, it must be here somewhere. On the third row, fourth shelf, stood a small bottle, all but tucked behind another. The label read RU 486.

Why shoved all the way back there?

Without spending another second thinking about it, Jess snatched the bottle. Relief flooded her as the sound of pills jostling around came from inside. She climbed over the counter and dashed up the stairs. Five minutes later and she knelt outside, covering the closed window with snow.

March 2025

Jess pointed to the three large lithium batteries fastened to the wall in the basement of her house. Mary's brow furrowed as a third green light on the side of one of them lit up.

"Those are our power cells." She moved her finger to the thick cable going through the wall. "Line feed from the solar panels on the roof to the converters." Then she traced a line from the cells to the fuse panel. "And the feed into the house circuit."

Mary nodded. "I don't know a lot 'bout electricity, but it looks impressive. Why do you keep your lights off all the time?"

Jess smiled. "So the militia don't grow suspicious."

Mary's brow arched and her eyes opened wide. "If they saw so many lights on, they would wonder how, because the block is under restricted electricity."

"Right." Jess pointed to the plants strewn about the basement floor. "I keep enough plants growing here to offset our food. What you don't see is the trap."

"Trap?" Mary asked.

"Yes, trap." Jess walked to the freezer on the north side of the basement. "Your father is letting you stay here, so it's important to know everything about this house." She stepped to the left of the freezer and reached behind it. "What I'm about to show you is a secret Mark created years ago, probably a few weeks after we bought the place." A click echoed. "There is a switch just behind the freezer, and a little push..." She put her shoulder down and shoved. The freezer screeched across the floor. A small door, no more than two feet high and across, stood before them.

"Hidden, as in hidden door." Mary laughed. "What's behind there?"

Jess lifted the wooden door. "Want to find out?"

April 2025

Jess grinned as Mark ran toward her on his short, chubby legs. His feet made slapping sounds on the hardwood floor of the living room. Mary laughed, as he let out a squeal of delight.

"Ma! Ma! Ma!" He slowed, hands reaching out to balance himself on a chair.

"Oh, look at you!" Jess bent and picked up her son, kissing him loudly on the cheek. "You're growing fast! Soon you'll be lifting me in the air."

Mark giggled and wiggled in her arms. "Ma we ha!" His smile widened on his face.

Jess smothered the child with kisses.

Mary got off the floor. "Did you get anything today?"

"Oh, you are sooooo big!" Jess laughed. "You can clean the two rabbits."

"Wabie!"

Jess put Mark back on the floor, and he ran into the living room. Even in these hard times, every child I've seen seems to have chubby legs. "Two, left them hanging in the garage, out of sight of the militia." She pulled off her white camo coat. "I swear they took the last one I caught."

"Probably." Mary grabbed the coat and went to the closet to hang it up. "I did see some prints before the snow came down." She closed the closet. "Did you know it's warming up?"

"Have you been listening to the short wave again?" Jess pulled off her boots.

Mary's cheeks reddened. "Yes."

"Mary!" Jess rubbed her forehead. "Did you at least hide the antenna?"

"Of course. I'm young, not stupid." She went to the patio door and pulled back the curtain. "Look, you don't even see the cable going up the tree."

Jess went to the door and stared at the snow. "You covered your tracks well." The tree reached up into the sky. Jess squinted at a little bit of cable, but it disappeared in the tangle of limbs. She tried to see the antenna. "Where is it?"

"Look up." Mary pointed near the top of the tree. "I placed it in the topmost branches I could reach."

"Mary! That's dangerous." It must be over ten metres up. "What'd happen if you fell?"

"Then I would crawl back into the house and wait for you." Mary reached down and picked up Mark who'd joined them in the kitchen. His little hand let go of her pants as she raised him up. "Anyways, Mark held the ladder."

"Not funny." Jess turned to the girl. Girl, more like young woman. She's over eighteen now, but I need to make sure she doesn't kill herself. "Anything like this should be the both of us doing it. That way, if something happens, the other can help."

Mary leaned her head on Jess's shoulder. "Then you would have climbed the tree and made me hold the ladder."

"It's my radio. Are you going to leave the antenna in the tree?" The white of the antenna stuck up from a line of snow against the tree. If she didn't know what to look for, she wouldn't have seen it.

"I just needed to do something." Mary took a few steps toward the kitchen. "You're so self-sufficient. I feel like I'm holding you back from doing something important." She opened a drawer, then closed it. "I do nothing but help a little in the kitchen and eat. I want to do something more than just survive."

Jess nodded. I knew something like this would happen.

Mary came up behind Jess and hugged her. "You've done so much for me, and now I want to help you."

"But you do help me." Jess pulled away, then faced the young woman. "You take care of Mark for me."

"And how long will that happen for? The way he's growing and moving about, well, he'll be helping you soon."

"What do you want to do?"

Mary's eyes widened. "I want to learn how to hunt."

June 2025

Jess held the 10/22 ready as Mary sighted down the barrel of the .17 cal. The morning air of the forest held no moisture today, and it caused the small hairs in her nose to freeze. The white coats and pants they wore helped hide their existence from the animals they hunted, and the searching eyes of the militia.

They travelled for an hour to reach this spot, leaving Mark with Bill MacDonald, and a promise of a share in what they caught. Bill had smiled as Jess told him they were both hunting today. He also thanked Jess for all she'd done for his once small girl who believed she was a victim and burden.

"Do you see it?" Jess asked.

"I think so." Mary adjusted the sight on the rifle. "It's about fifteen metres in front of us?"

Jess stared through her own scope. "Seventeen. Remember the drop and wind will affect the bullet. Not by much, but enough."

The rabbit dug into the snow, trying to reach what little grass lay dormant on the ground. The white fur hardly contrasted against the snow it burrowed into.

Jess counted. "Remember, deep breath through your mouth, hold for two seconds, then slowly release through the nose. Through the hold and exhale you're the steadiest you'll ever be. Adjust and squeeze the trigger—"

The retort of a rifle sounded in the distance. Snow and dirt flew in the air. The rabbit darted into the bush.

"Shit!" Mary started to stand.

Jess pulled her back down by an arm.

"You don't know who shot that." She examined the wound in the ground and followed it back to the source. A BV-206, well over a hundred metres away, rolled forward in the snow on wide tracks. Black smoke billowed out behind the thing as it darted left and right avoiding invisible trees.

"Who is it?" Mary asked.

"Militia." Jess lowered her rifle, closing the scope cap. "Close the cap and keep low."

The carrier, tracks digging up the snow and throwing it behind, came to a halt just a few metres before the hole in the ground. Don jumped out. His legs strained as they buckled under his belly. How did he get so big?

Don trudged forward, his feet sinking into the deep snow while he climbed the small hill. As he crested the top and approached the damaged ground, he cursed. "Fuck! Shit! Goddamn!"

A second person exited the jeep. He landed softly on his feet. The man towered over the fat Don and shook his head. "You really need to learn how to fire a rifle." He stepped forward to stand beside the fat man. "Look, you keep getting larger and larger rifles, but it is not the problem."

"God damn, Captain, I swear I had the thing."

"So where's the blood? The inevitable bone and splatter that cannon would have left?"

Don shouldered the BMG. The muzzle towered over his head, but not as tall as the Captain. "Maybe the fucking thing disintegrated?"

The Captain reached out and slapped Don. "I told you to watch your

41

language when around me." His voice punctuated every word.

Don stood there, staring at the Captain. His left hand clenched and unclenched. Lips pursed together. Head shook. Eyebrows knitted to form one straight line.

The Captain turned his back on the fat man. "I'm taking away your hunting fun, Don." He took off a glove. "You're reckless, wasteful, and uncouth. I'm also reassigning you."

Don unslung his rifle, pulled the bolt back and slammed it forward again. The tall man stopped, glove in hand. He slowly looked back.

"Really?" The Captain took off his cap. "You think this is a good move for you?"

"You've hit me for the last time," Don spat. "Every fucking time–"

"Language, Don."

"I don't give a shit! You're a fucking prude!" He braced the weapon against his shoulder.

The Captain shook his head. "Don, think about this for a second." His hands went into his overcoat pockets. "We left camp in the BV, everyone saw you carrying the BMG. They all know I need to keep an eye on you. If you return without me, what are you going to say?" He faced sideways and started to pace back and forth as if lecturing. "The best you could hope for is a cold cell wearing little clothes. The worse, stripped and buried in the snow up to your neck. It's your choice."

"Fuck you!"

The Captain stopped. "Put that thing down, Don."

"Fuck you!"

"I said, put the weapon down no–"

Jess jerked as Mary's rifle fired. A second report sounded ahead, almost as fast as the first. The Captain flew away from Don in slow motion. The fat man stared. A bullet ricocheted off the jeep window. Don threw his rifle down. He stumbled back and fell on his ass.

"What have you done?" Jess whispered. When she glanced toward Mary, the girl stared through her scope, pulling the trigger on the .17 cal. "Mary, you fired the round. You'll need to reload in order to shoot again." She reached out and put a hand on the bolt. "Why?"

Tears ran down Mary's face, brow knitted together, lips in a tight line. She portrayed that of a person battling an inner demon. "He's the one who raped me!" she hissed.

They waited until Don jumped into the tracked vehicle and sped away.

Once out of sight, Jess and Mary ran to the Captain only to find him dead. They left, travelling through the woods, underbrush, and finally made it home.

The snow fell to the ground around them. Not a heavy fall, but light, unlike the usual snowfall in June. Jess outpaced Mary and slowed to allow her to catch up. They approached the outskirts of town and slowed to a walk, keeping off the road in favour of the railroad tracks behind their home.

As they crawled toward the house, Jess caught a glimpse of action on the street. Three jeeps parked in the driveway, and one outside of the MacDonald's—Mary's parents' home. Jess motioned for a quiet approach, and Mary followed her lead.

From the tracks behind the home, Jess watched through the patio door with Mary as men stirred about the inside. Some glanced through the upper windows moving about and searching. The sound of crashes echoed out into the yard, and she wondered how they could hear such. A chair erupted through one of the second story windows. Jess held Mary back from rushing forward.

"Mark!" Mary said.

"Is with your parents, remember?" Jess pulled back her hand. "It's just a house." A small tear glistened in her eye.

They waited. Three shots echoed. Someone hurtled a black box out the window. The shortwave! Jess's heart shrank. The only way to contact anyone outside their town now destroyed. One of the last things Mark had purchased for them before the snow started in April. She sniffed back tears.

After an hour, smoke started to escape the upper window, and the militia poured from the house, jumping into their tracked vehicles. Jess bit her lip as the vehicles drove away.

"I've lost my home." Jess held back the anger and sense of loss. Now was not the time to think about it. "We'll sneak over to your parent's home. Find out what happened."

Mary nodded.

The MacDonald's front door hung at an odd angle, allowing snow to drift in. A quick look in the living room showed a trail of blood snaking into the kitchen. Too much blood. They followed it and found Mary's father sprawled on the kitchen floor, red pooled around him from a gash in his belly. The ripped flesh showed a wound inflicted at close

43

range with a sharp object.

Then, the sound of weeping reached them. Jess heard it first, but Mary located the source. She stood, whipped away the tears, and ran to a door opposite to where they entered. It led to the basement.

Before Jess could stop her, Mary ran down the stairs. Jess followed, unslinging her rifle. She stopped at the foot of the stairs and, instead of lifting it, let her left hand release its grip as the barrel dropped to point at the ground. Mrs. MacDonald lay on the floor, blood circled away from her toward the floor drain. Mary knelt beside her, holding a limp hand. She did not utter a sound, but the girl's shoulders heaved up and down sharply.

Mary's oldest sister crawled from behind a pile of wood, dragging one leg behind her. She pulled herself forward, face puffy and swollen, purple blotches almost making one solid colour. Two dark spots showed missing teeth from behind puffy, bloody lips. One swollen eye blinked, and the other did not open.

"M—M—Mary, they t—t—took Jilly and M—M—Mark."

"Who?" Jess asked. "Who took Mark?"

"The creep D—D—Don." She dropped fully to the floor, no longer moving.

Mary crawled to her sister, weeping uncontrollably.

"He's l—l—leaving. Said something about g—g—going south. He'll torture Jilly, probably M—M—Mark as well."

Grabbing her sister by the shoulders, Mary turned her over. Blood trickled from her mouth and nose. Some dripped out of her ear. "Find them…"

Jess slung her backpack on and strapped her 10/22 to it. She holstered two glock .17s and fastened down the catches. The map tacked on the wall showed the only route Don could take with the tracked jeep.

"He'll move slow, avoid any problem areas," Mary said.

"I know." Jess finished checking the map.

"We'll stay on the road side. Try and get something to catch up with him."

Jess zipped up her coat, pulled the map off the wall and folded it. "You're not coming with me."

"The hell I'm not."

"I made up my mind. You're not going with me."

"You can't stop me."

Jess faced Mary. The young woman, already dressed, stood determined in front of her. Emotion did not show, just a stare daring the other to deny the statement.

"We need to move fast."

"I know."

"We'll need to be self-sufficient."

"You taught me well."

Jess ran out of reasons. Hell, I don't want to do this alone. "Then let's go get Mark and Jilly."

The two women left the house, allowing the full moon to light their way as they sought a goal beyond their abilities to reach.

Snow in April – This story is a preview of an upcoming novel.

DRAGON

The morning sun glinted off Ka'lin's bronze scales as he gripped the rock shelf of the cave opening. A female inside emitted a musky scent, telling him the mating time was upon her.

His rear left claw held the body of a man, freshly killed, blood not yet drained. With his wing claws, Ka'lin pulled his bulky mass up, neck extending into the dark cave opening, nostrils flaring wide. Another sharp scent wafted to him, but so light he ignored it. The desire to mate took hold, driving the thoughts of why the female did not croon out of his mind. He pulled air into his massive lungs, held shut his fire bladder, and bellowed out in the Draconian language, "I am Ka'lin, from the mountains north of your range. You are in need of a mate, and I bring fresh meat for you to judge me."

He folded back the wing membranes and used his small fore claws to balance himself, taking care not to pulverise the body clenched in his back foot. She would judge his hunting skills based on how fresh and neatly killed the man appeared. Looking back, he made sure only the head lulled at the unnatural angle. The tail strike he used to kill the man showed precision and mastery at hunting.

In a hopping three-legged gait forced on him by the prize, he entered the cavern. The almost rancid underlying scent grew stronger, creating the first doubt in his mind that this was not a normal encounter. But the female smelled fresh and ready, so he proceeded inward.

"I am Ka'lin, from the mountains north of your range. Come forward to judge my kill and worthiness to be your mate."

His head cocked sideways, nostrils flaring once again as he sniffed at the air. Something definitely struck him as odd. A female in this condition should have rushed forward and screamed back either to demand the meal or challenge him. Nothing. He snaked his tongue out to taste the air. Metallic. Fishy. Something familiar, but not. His great horns waved back and forth as he shook his head. Then the glint of something deep inside the cave caught his eye.

Ka'lin, the mating drive overpowering his mind, rushed forward, believing light shone off the scales of a silver. She would be a prize. Silvers always bred strong dragon kind. With his seed in her, many eggs would come forth. Bronze and Silver, a perfect match.

Nonsensical shouting split the air. A heavy weight pulled his head toward the floor and he rolled. He lashed out with sharp teeth. "Who dares!" Extending one wing claw he tugged at what held him. The yelling of nonsense continued as men climbed out from behind rocks.

The men grabbed ropes and heaved. Ka'lin snapped at the binding. A mesh twisted round his head and fore wings. He thrust out a hind leg, letting the body fly toward his attackers. A deep inhale filled his lungs, and he readied to loosen his fire bladder. Something encircled his muzzle and tightened. It closed with a chomp. His fire bladders clamped tight.

Ropes encircled his wings and back claws, pulling and stretching him. He howled a muffled cry from deep in his throat, but through muzzled jaw only a whimper escaped. The men yanked on the ropes. One of them clambered onto his back. He wiggled, furious at the insult, but the man grabbed his back spikes. Used them to make a way to his neck where he dropped a noose.

Ka'lin tried to gulp air, but only a trickle came through. He tugged against the ropes, but the men had them tightened around large, heavy rocks. Knowing nothing could free him, Ka'lin let his body go limp, hoping for a quick death.

Pain lanced through his head. The world went dark.

Ka'lin's body jolted, and he woke. His head pounded. He attempted to stretch, but his legs and wings would not move. He wanted to stretch his neck, but something blocked his head from moving forward. He tried to yawn, but ropes bit into his muzzle. Lifting his eyelids took concentration, and his spinning head did not afford much of that. Bindings held him down, keeping him from shaking his body, and affording him little movement.

Sharp words spoken in the language the men issued throughout the cave. Ka'lin opened his eyes, expecting blinding light. Nothing. The world showed blackness. He scrunched heavy brows, and a small amount of light crept into his vision on the top and bottom of his eyes. Blindfolded. An attempt to take a deep breath made bindings bite into his side. He pushed against them, but only filled his lungs with a small breath of air laced heavy with horse smell. As he released his breath, a small whimper escaped. Then he caught scent of the female. She must be close.

Ice touched his side, and he recoiled. The small spot made its way along his body and to the great shoulder muscles that powered his wings. A tug at the bindings proved why his wings could not extend. The spot crawled along his scale-covered skin until finally the form of a man stood in his sight. Ka'lin took in a sharp breath.

"I am Ka'lin, from the mountains to the north. If you release me, I will not eat you." He flared his nostrils, exhaling hot breath.

The man kept examining the ropes. Ka'lin grunted when the bindings holding his muzzle were tugged. Apparently satisfied, the man turned away and called out to someone behind Ka'lin.

Metal clanked and boots stomped. Soon several men in glinting suits of metal walked up and stood to either side of his head. Ka'lin slowly levelled his gaze from one to the other. I will eat the fat one first, then the short one. None stood in front of his mouth.

The wisp of robes drew his attention to the right, and a figure clad in dark cloth, face obscured, strode up to his muzzle, though over to one side like the guards. It carried a long stick affixed with an ordinary rock. Long silver hair flowed out of the hood and down the front. The being had to be a female from its small stature.

"Hello, Ka'lin," the figure said in the grumbling tongue of Dragon kind.

Surprise welled in Ka'lin, but he kept his eyes steady. How such a small creature could intone the deep sounds of a dragon, he did not know. He stared at the figure, trying to pierce the hooded darkness.

"I am Ka'lin, from the mountains to the north. I would give you my lineage, but you do not introduce yourself properly to have such an honour." He snorted, wishing the ropes were a little less tight.

"My name is of no consequence, dragon. You are a prize to be milked for the fire inside." He motioned behind him. "I would guess your fire bladder is very full by now, what with all the excitement a few days ago…"

Two men came from behind hauling a wooden contraption. The machine rolled on small wheels. Its front, a long cylinder with a sharp

49

point at the end, came to rest in front of Ka'lin's face.

"I'll be loosening your muzzle ropes. Don't try to breathe fire, for you will not be able to lift your head to get a good gulp of air." The man motioned again, and this time two guards on each side of Ka'lin came forward. They made quick work of whatever held the ropes in place. The pressure relaxed. Ka'lin opened his mouth. The contraption came forward, ramming into his jaw. He gagged as the thing made its way down his throat, growing taller the deeper it went. His eyes watered. Dots of green and blue filled his vision. He attempted to cough, but could not take in enough air. Thoughts of suffocating spun through his mind.

Ka'lin struggled, but the ropes across his muzzle were only loosened, and the ones across his body still held tight. Two spikes of pain erupted in his throat. His fire bladder bulged and threatened to split. The men on the machine turned a wheel at its end, and a sucking sounded in Ka'lin's throat. If he had food in his stomach, it would have made its presence known. Fortunately for the men, his stomach was empty.

The pain subsided. The machine creaked back out of his mouth, and as it rolled back, Ka'lin noticed it had split across. Inside the hollow log cowered a child. He snapped at the child, and the ropes tightened.

"Food for our guest," said the form, then sputtered something in the human language.

Ka'lin's stomach grumbled. He didn't know how long it'd been since food passed through his jaws.

One man came forward carrying a thick coil. He grabbed Ka'lin's nose and shoved the rope into it. The thing snaked down, stinging with every shove unit it hit his throat. He started to swallow, to get it out of his nasal passage, but the man kept pushing it in.

It settled into his stomach and soon food fell into his belly, but he was too uncomfortable. A shout and his head lowered. The man hauled the rope out of his nasals, and it came out with a sucking noise, covered in mucus. Ka'lin's nose burned.

"Maybe, if you're lucky, you'll eat real meat sometime." The form spun, then walked back the way he came.

They travelled for a week. Men rode and horses pulled the cart Ka'lin and the silver rode on. Every day the man came, running his hand up Ka'lin's neck. On the third and sixth day after his visit, they brought out the machine and drained his fire bladder. The cloaked figure showed every time, talking to Ka'lin and telling him to keep filling his fire bladder.

On the seventh night, Ka'lin's legs and back started to itch, his wings cramped up, and he wanted so desperately to lite to the air. Bound and drained, he dreamed about freedom, racing through the sky, air under his wings, and hunting.

"You must keep producing," came a soft voice in Dracon, the language of Dragons. "If you stop, they will kill and eat you."

Ka'lin rotated his ears to locate the speaker, behind him, to the left. It must be the silver. "And what if I decide not to?" His voice came out gruff and rumbly, his throat sore from the last milking. "Then how can we escape?"

It was sensible. If he forced his body to stop filling the fire bladder then the humans would find him useless. But how could so few eat all of his bulk, it didn't make sense.

"And how can we escape?"

A slight prumming sounded in the air. The female must be rumbling her breath in her lungs. "At the right time clamp down during the milking. They will struggle to pull the small one inside away. You must keep it in your mouth without killing it. They are the children of the guards, so none will injure the child for fear of vengeance."

"But they push it in too fast." Ka'lin could not imagine trying to crush a log.

"You'll know when they are starting, just turn your head and clamp down when they start pushing it in."

"And then?" He pondered the possibility.

"Once the child is secure, you can demand the father release your bonds with the promise of the child's safe return."

A stellar idea. "They will milk me again in two suns." He glanced skyward, but the humans always pointed him to the north. "And you? Will you be loosened for the world?"

"I am but young."

"No, you are ready to have a clutch." Ka'lin strained against the ropes. The scent of her readiness to mate still lingered on his tongue. "Only a grown one of our kind could flavour the air as you do."

"I have never breathed fire." She sighed. "The only reason they keep me is to lure others of our kind."

"How many have they captured?"

"A claw's worth that I know of, maybe more."

Four. These men have captured four or more and killed them when

51

they willed their fire bladders empty. Ire built up in Ka'lin. Men live only a short span of years in comparison to dragon kind. "Why did you not escape with the others?"

A small whimper sounded before she responded. "I am young. The"—she said a word he could not understand—"raised me from the egg. This is all the life I've known. The last one talked about flying. He described the sensation of wind under the wings. The thrill of the hunt. Basking in the sun on a mountain top. It was then that my wings ached, and they bound them that night."

"Then you are very young." Ka'lin prummed. "You have many eggs to raise before age takes you." Fire rose in his loins at the thought of mating the female, blood boiled in cold veins. His fire bladder, tender as it may be, pulsed as it filled. "I think they will try to milk me tomorrow. We will escape at that time.

A cold hand came up his neck, pausing where the fire bladder bulged under the skin and scales. Ka'lin smiled to himself, in an hour he would be free.

The hand left his skin, and several wing beats later the sound of a now familiar voice grated on the wind. "You filled fast this time." A hand touched his neck. Unlike the others, this one warmed the area. "Something you ate?" Laughter, then coughing broke the day.

"Why not loosen my bonds and look to see?" He imagined chomping down on the weak figure, breaking bones and splitting the body in half with a mighty bite.

"I may just do that," the figure said, coming into view. It appeared slumped as if the weight of something horrible lay on its shoulders.

Ka'lin cared not why, but only wanted the thing to order the milking so he could escape. The figure grunted something in the human tongue and stepped forward, laying a hand on the armoured snout of his captive.

"One day we will see how well you fly." It lifted a hooded head. Scales glinted in the late evening sun and slitted eyes stared out at him. White hair draped down over the face.

A wizard!

The small capsule rolled up and bonds loosened just enough for Ka'lin to part his jaw. Forward it inched. The front spikes on top and bottom jabbed, so he opened his mouth. A little more, and the thing would be on his tongue. Now!

He spun his head, tilting the world. Jaws came down, crunching against the unprotected sides of the instrument. A scream pierced the air. The hands of a man beat against his neck. The bonds fell. His neck, now free, ached to arch. Ka'lin raised up, lifting the thing into the air. A small object the size of a child slid to the top of his tongue. He used the muscle to hold it there while the wood fell to the ground.

Ka'lin smiled. It caused the men around him to freeze. A man, not tall but muscled as some of their kind are, stepped forward and fell to his knees, hands clasped in front of him. Gibberish in their tongue spewed from his mouth.

"He asks that you spare his child." The cloaked figure glared at the groveling man and spoke in their tongue.

Saliva pooled in Ka'lin's mouth as he held the child. "Cut me loose."

The man stood and rushed forward, hand pulling a dirk from sheath.

"Catilata!" yelled the hooded figure.

The man froze; one hand on a rope and the other ready to slice through with the knife. "Matalinta, Ma' sill catilata pottoona Ma'," he whimpered back.

The figure took a deep breath that hissed through tight lips. "If we free you, the child must be let free."

"Agreed." A sour taste touched his tongue. "And the silver is to be freed as well."

The wizard spun, let out a short command, and one of the men broke off from the group and approached the silver dragon. "You will not get far with her," the wizard said. It turned to Ka'lin.

"And why not?" Ka'lin spied the thin, green lips under the hood smiling.

"She cannot fly."

Confussion ran though Ka'lin's mind. A dragon that could not fly was unheard of. Dragons needed to be free, to feel the wind under their wings. If she did not fly, how could she mate? They are not animals who just did it anywhere. The fear of his escape with her started to tear apart.

"How is this so? She appears healthy and strong. The mating scent is about her as well. What have you done to her?" A rope slid off Ka'lin's body, and he flexed a stiff wing, bringing blood back to the powerful limb.

"I acquired her as an egg," responded the wizard. "She has never flown. The muscles in her back are not strong enough for flight."

"Free her anyway." The last of the ropes released and he stretched out a back leg, claws grating against the wagon he sat upon.

The wizard chuckled. "There are chains in her wings. Even if she could lift herself, they will make a racket for all to hear. She will not be able to hunt."

"We'll take our chances."

Ka'lin watched closely as the bindings came off the female. His mouth, now fouled by the child, needed washing. Soon the female, freed from her bonds, stretched out her legs and wings. He spied chains grown into the thin membrane of her wings. They glinted in the sun, having been sheltered in the wing folds. He grunted.

"I will release the child before lifting. Stand back, for we are walking away a few tail spans to be safe from you." He stepped off the cart, glancing toward the figure. "And you. I will be singing this to my kind as far as my wings may take me."

Ka'lin swore he saw steam rise from the wizards head, but a quick shake removed the image and elicited a sharp squeal from the captive in his jaws. He walked, keeping his attention behind him, toward a small clearing. The silver, already waiting for his arrival, used her teeth to tug at one of the chains in her wings.

Once with her, Ka'lin lowered his mouth and released the child from inside. It scampered a few feet before he reached out a great taloned wingtip and halted the retreat. "You will stay here until we fly." He then felt silly, the child just stared at him blankly, body tensed and ready to run once again. Another faint smell of waste filled the air, and he looked down. The child had fouled himself again. Well, at least it was not in his mouth this time.

"Are you ready?" he asked the silver.

She lifted a wing and a jingle erupted for a second. "My wings are heavy, but I believe a short flight might work."

Ka'lin lifted his head. "There is water to the south. Probably just a few wing beats away. We'll head in that direction. I need to remove the taste of human foul from my mouth."

The silver prummed, her wings beat at the air, and with agonizing slowness she lifted into the sky.

"As for you!" Ka'lin bellowed, eyes narrowing on the figure and guards. "I want to make sure you do not follow." He took in a deep breath, opened his mouth wide and let his fire bladder empty.

The silver did not fly fast, nor did she climb very high into the air. Ka'lin approached from above, swooping down beside her and beat his wings to slow. The land spanned before them, showing the tops of trees for miles. The sun warmed the earth, making updrafts that hit one of the silver's wings, causing her to go off course. He would need to show her how to ride the rising air and conserve energy. One of many things he would teach her. But first, he thirsted for water and desired to rinse his mouth clean.

He glanced at the silver pounding her wings in the air. The female's breathing was laboured, and her green eyes only slits in the otherwise beautifully scaled face. They would need to land soon, her strength not anywhere near his due to a life of captivity and those metal chains in her wings.

"There," he called out. "Do you see the large opening before us?"

"I only– see– green– and gray," she puffed.

Exhaustion. The one killer of dragons. She would keep flying, beating her wings, and fall out of the sky unable to stop herself if they did not land.

"Only a few beats more. Extend your wings. Feel the air lift you as the sun is in the sky."

Ka'lin watched as the silver extended her wings to glide, but the weight of the chains dragged against the membrane of her wings, pulling her down toward the canopy of trees.

"Beat your wings!" Ka'lin bellowed. "Only a little bit farther!"

She did as told. Ka'lin imagining the strain. He remembered his first flight. How far Father had made him fly. The burning of his back. But this would make her stronger. When we break the chains, her strength will be astounding.

Ka'lin's talon's bit into the soft sand beside the silver. He rode her scent all the way down, ensuring she landed safely. The sand about her showed the impact of her landing, and some of it stuck to her under-scales with the wetness of the water. No huts or homes decorated the shoreline. This made Ka'lin happy. He did not want to battle humans just yet.

"Drink, I need to clean." Lowering his head into the water, Ka'lin opened his mouth and swished back and forth. Soon, the foul taste of the child left his mouth. Taking three great gulps, he satisfied his thirst.

A splash made him lift his head. The silver, now half in the water, jumped and spat wisps of flame at the water. Her actions reminded him of a small, furry animal that wandered into his lair many years ago. Its claws, sharp but very short, could grab onto his scales as it pounced on his flicking tail. The creature did not last long, unfortunately. It did eat a lot of mice, though.

"What are you doing?" Ka'lin asked.

"Something touched my leg." The silver leapt again. "There! Did you see it?"

Ka'lin glanced at the water, then thrust his head under the surface, snapping. The taste of blood filled his mouth, and he lifted his head up.

"A big fish," he said, and whipped his head to throw the thing onto the shore. It thudded to the ground.

"I have never seen the like," Silver said, walking up the beach. She stared at the fish. "Do... do we eat it?"

"That or we can wait until the birds squawk so loud that we lose our hearing." He looked at the sky. "We only have a few beats to devour it."

"You caught it, you take it." The silver nudged the fish.

"No," he said. "The prize is yours." He strolled up beside her. "My desire is for us to be together." Ka'lin rubbed his frill against the side of her neck.

"You are kind, but I am a burden." She lifted a wing, and the tinkle of the chains rang across the shore. "I have no way of flying for any type of mating or journey. We are lucky I made it this far."

Ka'lin nosed at the chains, sniffed, and nibbled a little. Their metal surface scratched from his teeth and tasted off, like the taste of man. "I fear a Wizard's hand in the making of these."

"The cloaked one," she said, pulling back her wing.

"Yes, the cloaked one." Ka'lin shook his head, then rubbed against her gently. "We will find a way."

Ka'lin hunted during the fading light when day became night. He ranged farther every day, scouring the land for food and information. When he came across a settlement he would wait until it was dark, then sneak in to find a blacksmith. Each time the men ran in fear of their lives. "Dragon!" they would cry, or "Beast!"

He worried that freeing the silver could be beyond his ability. But the pang of desire for her ran deep through him. And desire meant climbing high into the sky, then twisting their bodies together while plummeting to the earth. He would find a way.

One village came into view. Larger than the others, the cluster of homes boasted a spanning fort in the middle with fields aplenty. He landed just at the tree line as the last rays of sun slipped from the sky. Being quiet in his steps, he scanned for the tell tale signs of a blacksmith: smoke and coal. After several moments, he sighted the whisping of smoke from a great forge near a small hut. It would be the blacksmith.

The tree line hid his form in shadows of darkest black, even with a full moon hanging in the sky. Ka'lin stalked his way to the forge, poking his head into the small area and getting a snout full of smoke. A small figure, smaller than the child he once held in his maw, stood to the side with an empty bucket. Small eyes challenged the moon's size as it gazed at him. One hand reached up to point, and a mouth opened then closed.

"I mean no harm," Ka'lin said, eyebrows raised and head lowered to the ground. "I am just an honest dragon looking for help."

The child's mouth clamped shut. It tilted its head to the side. A smile came across small lips, and it spoke with the most absurd accent Ka'lin had ever heard. "Scaled kitty smoke mouth."

His grin started to reveal teeth, but he quickly closed his lips when its brow danced upward, showing eyes larger than the world. He switched tongues and decided dragon speak would not be correct for this encounter. He remembered flying over elven lands, so decided to speak High Elf, hoping the child knew the tongue. "Are you the blacksmith's offspring?"

It dropped the pail and clapped. "Yes, I am, dragon, sir."

Ka'lin allowed his head to rest on the ground, indicating no desire to attack. "I am in need of your father's services, but I am concerned he will be angry or frightened if he sees me."

"Father trades with the dragons of the North. He has never been harmed by them and says they are nicer than the people of the village sometimes." One finger pointed to a pile of shields at the other end of the forge. "He gets scales for shields. Says they are better than beaten metal."

Ka'lin stared at the pile, the aged scales showed no blood from being ripped off a body. "Your father must be a kind man. May I speak to him?"

The child nodded. "Stay here, I'll be back." Then it ran off into the home.

Ka'lin didn't have to wait long. A door opened, and a man towering over the child came out into the night, carrying a lamp. His arms bulged like tied rope with no hair. He carried himself well for a man with many gray hairs upon his head. What surprised Ka'lin was the absence of any weapons. The man must be trusting, or know his way around dragons. But then again, he did not lack in weapons for many could be reached by hand for they lay all around the forge.

"You need a blacksmith, dragon?" The man spoke in the dragon tongue but carried the same queer accent as his daughter, dropping the r's and changing the d's to s's.

"Yes, blacksmith." Ka'lin bowed his eyes, then returned the stare.

"What do you need?" The man sat on the forge's edge, relaxing at the sound of Ka'lin's voice.

"My mate, a silver, has chain rings in her wings." Ka'lin raised his head to make talking easier. "They keep her from flying any distance or mating."

"Wing rings," the blacksmith said. "I've seen them in a few of the dragons of the North, but they never really stop them from flying."

"These ones do." Ka'lin pictured the wings in his mind. "There are for talons of rings in each wing. The rings are a brownish silver as if kissed by bronze and iron. They are strong and taste strange."

"An alloy," the blacksmith said. "I've heard of such. The wizards of the Southern Reach are reported to be able to blend metals together to form stronger bindings that hold spells better."

Ka'lin nodded. "That could be. She was a captive of a Wizard."

"We need to get the rings out of her wings."

Ka'lin struggled to keep in the air with the blacksmith gripping tight to a rope. It took much convincing at first, but when the blacksmith warned that he himself could not fly, Ka'lin relented. The thick rope reached behind his neck, just in front of his great wings. The blacksmith did not cause the weight problem, the tools he insisted on bringing did. They weighed twice as much as the man, if not more, and Ka'lin's claws cramped from holding them.

He struggled to lift off, and once in the air his wings bulked under the weight. Flap after flap gained him little height until his shoulders burned. Then, when he almost dropped one of the bags, he reached a good distance from the earth and caught a thermal. The rising air afforded him time to relax and stretch his wings out while he circled. Soon they touched clouds, and the man yelled.

"The air is too cold and thin for me up here. We need to be closer to the earth!"

Ka'lin pulled back his wings and the world pulled him down. They flew for many beats of wings. And when the sun's light crested the world's edge, he dove for the shoreline. He released the tool bags first and flexed his clawed feet. The cramps relented, and with ease he landed. The blacksmith climbed off his back and stood beside him, one hand shaking in the air and the other smoothing back his hair.

"A fine flight, dragon."

"My name is Ka'lin, of the Northern Mountains." Ka'lin lifted his head high, causing a jutting out of the chest and his shinny copper scales to catch the light. "My silver seems to be hiding from you. Her experience with humans has always been one of slavery."

The man shook his head. "Such a shame. Man should work with all intelligent animals in order to better the world for all."

"An honourable statement. Unfortunately, not all men feel the same way you do." Ka'lin stepped forward. "I'll call for her." He took in a deep breath and let out a call in dragon speak so loud the man covered his ears.

A rustle of branches and the silver emerged onto the beach from several wing spans away. Leaves decorated the corner of her mouth until a quick tongue pulled them inside. She chewed as powerful legs bore her toward the two unlikely partners.

"This blacksmith agreed to take the rings out," Ka'lin said. "He is very skillful and requested the honour of helping us without challenge or threat. I wish more men were like he."

The man bowed to the silver, then raised his hands palms up. "I am a blacksmith of the town Rindward, and it will be my pleasure to release you."

The right brow of the silver raised, then she slowly extended a wing for the man to examine. He approached, running a hand gently over the smooth membrane until it encountered a ring of the chain. It punctured the soft skin just at the knuckle joint of the bone and three of the links after it did the same. Ka'lin stared as the man touched his soon to be mate. The tinkle of metal tapping metal lit the air.

"They're enchanted," the man said. "It will take a hot forge and probably a lot of pain." He shook his head. "I can't promise she will be able to fly after removing them."

"Whatever you can do, Master Blacksmith," the silver said.

"I can supply the hot forge," Ka'lin said. "Will dragon fire do?"

"Yes, if it is yours." The Blacksmith nodded.

"Then I will gather stone to build it." Ka'lin jumped into the air, spread his great wings, and climbed into the sky.

It took much of Ka'lin's strength and most of the morning, but twelve great stones and many small ones littered the sand near the trees. The Blacksmith also busied himself by digging clay and moving the rocks he could. The silver stacked the large boulders with the Blacksmith's direction.

Soon a respectable forge stood on the beach, and still the sun hung in the sky, though much lower than before.

Ka'lin spat fire on the sides of the forge to harden the clay, and the three unlikely companions made their way into the forest to collect wood. When the day gave way to night, the Blacksmith announced the work successful and held his grumbling stomach.

"I will catch fish for our meal," Ka'lin said and bounded into the air.

He flew over the water, diving in upon spying a fish and erupting out of the sea with the small creature in his talons. Once secured, he dropped the fish on the shoreline not far from the Blacksmith and went out again to find another. He repeated this ten times, catching enough for every member of their small group.

"This is a good meal," the Blacksmith said, turning one of the fish over the forge.

"Yes," replied the silver. "A fine meal."

"Tell me, Blacksmith—"

"My name's Jentar," he said.

"I'm sorry." Ka'lin bowed his head. "I should have asked you your name many wing beats ago."

"There is no harm." Jentar waved his hand. "We have the same goal, freeing the silver from her chains." He motioned toward the silver. "I would only ask one thing."

"Name it," both dragons said at the same time.

"Scales." Jentar stood. "I need scales for my armour and shields."

"How many?" Ka'lin glanced toward the silver.

Jentar rubbed his chin for a few seconds. "Say, one hundred scales over a year."

Ka'lin's brow furrowed. He added up how many scales he naturally shed in a year and how many the silver might. "Done. I promise one hundred scales over a year."

Jentar nodded. "I have known you but a short time, Ka'lin, but you seem to be a dragon of your word." He stretched, a great yawn taking hold of his face for a second. "The day grows late. I'll start on the chains tomorrow." As he stepped toward the forge, he turned an eye back to Ka'lin. "Will you supply more fish for tomorrow?"

Ka'lin shook his head. "I was thinking of hunting a deer."

The wind buffeted against Ka'lin's head as he swooped down into the clearing with talons extended. A scream cut the air as they bit into flesh, and he beat the air with his wings. Any successful hunt was a celebration, but this large deer would feed him, the silver, and the man for two days.

As he gained more height, the deer stopped struggling, all of its life emptied. With one talon tip, Ka'lin slit the beasts belly as he flew, like he'd done with many other deer in the past, and let the entrails fall from the animal.

One year, one hundred scales. The thought drove through his mind.

The small forge on the beach came into view, and Ka'lin stretched out his wings to land. Jentar, true to his word, worked on removing the rings that morning. Ka'lin watched in awe as he detached twenty of the links within an hour, and now it looked as if one wing flapped free of the heavy weights.

"I should be finished within the hour." Jentar wiped sweat from his brow. "I have a salve at my hut I think will help with the healing."

"You are a master Blacksmith, Jentar." The silver prummed. "I will forever be in your debt."

Jentar nodded, his hand reaching into the fold of her wing and touching the skin softly. "You are one of the most beautiful dragons I've had the pleasure to assist. And Ka'lin is definitely the most honourable."

Ka'lin motioned them over. "Come, the morning hunt was successful, and we have a deer for the fire."

He dropped the carcass by the forge and waited for Jentar to come and see the beast. The Blacksmith nodded, freed yet another ring, and stepped back. His gaze found the deer and black eyebrows peppered with gray arched to the sky. He reached down, unsheathed a small dirk from his belt, and cut the heart from the beast.

"Do you eat the heart?" he asked Ka'lin.

"Dragons eat all the beast except the entrails. We usually gut them in flight like I did."

"Did you want the heart?"

"No, you may do with it what you may."

Jentar took the heart to the silver and let her feast on it.

For the next hour, the deer cooked in the heat of the forge, Ka'lin tearing at a leg and the man slicing small pieces of meat as it became cooked. After each felt their fill, Jentar returned to his task of freeing the silver.

Ka'lin watched for several minutes but grew bored of the sounds. He first worried at the silver's hissing, but soon understood Jentar only worked at removing the rings. Not wanting to watch any more, he walked into the water and swam. He returned late in the day to find the forge cool and Jentar packing up his tools.

Ka'lin glanced about. "Where is the silver?"

"I am here," came a lilting voice very unlike the dragon Ka'lin referred to.

Ka'lin turned. "Where?"

"Here." A woman, young with long silver hair, full breasts, and slim waste stepped forward. Her hair cascaded down an otherwise naked body. "Ka'lin, I have been freed!"

"What trickery is this?" Ka'lin roared. His ears folded back, fire bladder bubbling. He caught the scent of the silver, but only the human woman stood near.

"No trickery," Jentar said. "Remember I told you the chain was enchanted? It was when I removed the last one that I discovered what the spell actually was." He tossed a chain link on the ground. "It is a transformation chain. This woman, probably when she was a child, had these woven into her arm, causing a transformation to a dragon. Probably by some very powerful wizard. Removing them freed her. You ordered the breaking of the chains, now she is free."

Ka'lin swooped down in the darkness on the small village and landed outside the home of Jentar. He folded his wings and dropped another ten scales onto the ground before nosing the bell mounted beside the door.

"Another ten," he said. "Only thirty more to go."

He wavered on weak feet and started to turn when the door flew open. Standing there in a flowing white gown stood Silver, her hair stirring softly in the slight breeze of the evening.

"Don't go," she said.

Ka'lin stopped his turn, but did not look at her. He wanted to stay, desired to. But humans cannot be trusted. "I must."

"Much has happened these last months, and I miss you."

"You are human, I am dragon. There is a debt to pay that I agreed to." He spread his wings.

"I miss you."

"And I miss who you were, but we are now of different worlds, and your chains no longer bind you to me."

He waited for another second, then jumped in the air, flying away, his scales glistening in the moonlight. Thoughts of a silver stirring in a memory filled with confusion and grief.

STITCHING

Icy claws pull back from my mind as light from the overhead bulb cuts away the fog. It hurts. I adjust, wiggling just a little to take away the sores from sleeping in the same position overnight. Or was it day? Time has slipped away. Is it Monday? Friday?

I stare at the ceiling, white and padded. Stitching races across it. I count. Five horizontal lines, ten vertical. The pattern runs up and down the walls as well as side to side. Once, I tried to chew a stitch loose. Now, they keep me secured to the bed with straps. Adult diapers allow me to shit and piss without getting up. The only good part about my situation is it keeps me from sleeping. The nightmares come when I sleep.

When did it happen? Not sure. I remember waking one morning, not knowing the nightmare was a nightmare. Joyce, that was her name. Yellow corn hair, eyes as blue as the morning sky, skin softer than a cat's stomach fur. A knife jutted from her chest. Red rivers tumbled down, making the bed sheets sticky. I cried that morning. The kids, oh the little angels, their throats smiled at me as the black bags zipped over their faces to hide the ashen white of their cheeks. Who would do such a thing?

The Judge's gavel slammed down, announcing how wicked and cruel the world was. His jutting finger thrust through the air as if a javelin of justice. Innocent due to insanity. But I am not insane. You see, it's the dreams.

When they saw me chewing the wall, nothing happened. I needed something to keep me awake back then. Not until I'd swallowed a few feet of thread did they come in. My arms, secured in the jacket, ripped at my body as I struggled to flail free. It almost worked.

That was when the doctor gave me my first shot.

I slept peacefully for the first time in years. No dreams. Blissful.

It's a dream.

My mind is playing tricks on me. Confusing me to think the memories are nothing, harmless. I know what dangers lurk in my dreams. It's when the monsters take over and bad things happen.

I defecate.

Darkness blankets my room. No one has changed my diaper. The smell of rancid feces mixes with the acid scent of urine fills my nostrils. Skin chafes and I know there will be sores later.

They hope my discomfort has weakened the resolve to escape the monsters in the dreams awaiting sleep, but I have a plan. Concentration, that is my defense, as well as contorting my neck as much as possible. The angle, hard to achieve while restricting bonds cut into my skin, causes pain to lance into my skull and runs a gambit between aching shoulder blades.

I fight to stay awake.

Time passes.

There is nothing to occupy my mind as a thin sliver of light creeps into the room from under the door. Room check.

I squint my eyes as a slide on the door slams aside. A column of brightness spills on the floor. Dust dances in the beam, and I start counting. Then a face appears, framed by brightness. Black and grey stubble adorn a rounded chin. Thick glasses magnify black eyes. A smile curls the corners of the mouth and a broken-toothed grin forms. A tongue darts out and licks the pale lips with slow deliberation.

I stare at the face as it pushes against the framed orifice in the door.

The opening stretches as the face mushes its way through. Glasses fold slightly then break, falling to the floor. Eyes once magnified now bulge. The tongue lances out and swipes the eyes clean. They're black. Darker than the darkest overcast night on a waning moon. A pop echoes through my small room. One of the shoulders is now through the opening. I watch as the face slides to the floor followed by a body bereft of bones.

A small puddle of skin and features pool on the ground as the door groans back into place. I lift my head and the figure reforms a solid head. Shoulders rise and the mess under them shrinks. A man forms. His large eyes stare at me from a head slowly turning red. Horns grow from his temples. Jagged spears reaching for the ceiling. The fire of ages smolder in the eyes.

He reaches for me, a clawed hand emanating heat burns against my throat. I scream.

White lights burn bright, hurting my eyes. The lock rattles. A thud announces the door hitting the wall. Many steps rush in and hands hold me down. Too many hands to count. I still scream.

A sharp pinch on my shoulder and fog floods into my mind. I stop struggling. Bindings are removed. My pants are pulled off, and I try to respond to the disturbed voices around me, but only gibberish comes out. This will make me sleep.

Uncaring hands strip off my clothes with rough efficiency. Cold, wet cloths send shivers over my body as they clean me. A retching sound followed by splashing fills the air, and the smell of sick grows thick.

I'm lifted from the bed and made to stand on legs that will not listen to my commands to run. A fresh mattress replaces the old one. How many times have they performed this action?

Clean sheets go on the bed, and hands pull me toward the it again. They push me down, arms at my side, legs straight. Straps are secured on my ankles and wrists. I cannot stop them. They work with the mechanical precision of a well-rehearsed dance.

The last of them tugs at the restraints and nods before he leaves the room. A slam announces the door closing. Rattling keys and the click of a lock sliding into place are the last things I remember before the lights go out.

Evil comes in all forms. I wait for mine in the fog of darkness and dreams. Years are long, especially when you're locked away inside a little room. You forget how to do things. Eat properly. Piss while standing. Wipe your ass. Talk without grunting. Be polite to a pretty girl. But nothing will keep the evil from my mind as I drift to sleep.

The lights come on.

I blink, wait for my eyes to adjust. Twist. Fall off the bunk.

Total surprise confuses me while I struggle to sit up. My legs are still bound but no longer on the bed. I pull at my arms, and one comes free of the bindings. A pang of disconnection hits me while I reach over and untie my other arm. Freedom.

I've not been free to move for years. They watch me. Make sure I sleep. But usually, I can confuse them, just as their needle confuses most patients in the building. Deftly, I untie my legs.

Knees creak, complain, buckle. It's been so long.

Stretch. Touch toes. Limber up. Be ready for anything. Don't let them bind you again.

Keys jingle, and the lock snaps back. I stare as the door swings open. He is there. Skin deep red like lava cooling on a warm day after erupting from the earth. His horns jut upward, the ends like needles in the sky. He smiles. A nod toward the hall tells me he wishes well, and I don't question it. I dart out.

Claxons bellow out around me, but I don't care. Screams, yells, and hooting follow me down the hall as I run faster than I've ever run before, trying to find freedom. The sky. I want to see the sky.

Pain stabs into my back. Skin pulls. Another stab and more pulling. I look behind to see hooks in my flesh tied to ropes. The demon laughs from behind me and yanks back. I scream.

Lights stir me from slumber. I taste copper, and my tongue hurts. The dreams again. An acidic scent tells me more than the wetness between my legs. They would come in again. I wait. Count the stitching in the ceiling.

Time passes. How much, I don't know. The stretch of one's existence is measured in heartbeats. One a second. Two a second. Three a second.

Pain!

Blood gushes from my chest.

A hand erupts and claws at my face.

I scream.

Dizziness.

The world floats around me.

I open sluggish eyes and look about. The padded walls stare back at me. The stitching is coming loose in places. Small lines of curling thread dropped from above to draw a connection to nothing in the air.

A world of change is happening. Those once white padded walls now gray with ding and dirt.

The door, once closed and locked, now ajar. He stands there, smiling, one finger extended only to curl it back to me. An inviting gleam in those smoldering red eyes.

I am not bound.

Freedom awaits.

I sit up. Swing sore legs over the bed's edge and stand. He chuckles so lightly I can barely hear it. Then, a deep rumbling base. The floor shakes with that laughter. An ending to an imperfect life.

There is no hesitation. No reluctance. Only three regrets. The children and wife. No more dreams. This is an escape from them.

I walk toward the door. Head swinging down. Feet shuffling.

The light is bright behind him. His long arm comes out and rests on my shoulder. It weighs nothing. The frustrations of days gone by leave my sole.

I step past him. Into the light.

"It's done." Father MacTavish closed his bible and took a heavy breath. "His soul is released from this world and now is with Our Lord."

A nurse reached up and switched off the ECG, EEG, and respirator. She bowed her head, causing folds of skin to bulge out. After a second, she glanced up at the tall, slender woman sitting beside the bed, holding a lifeless hand. "I'll leave you alone with him—"

"No. Please, I'll only be a second." Brenda reached up and brushed her hair away from a face covered in the thin white lines of healed wounds. A tear welled up in one eye, and mindlessly she dabbed at it with a tissue. "You bastard."

Father MacTavish blushed. "I'll take my leave of you, Mrs. Boarden."

"Ms."

"I'm sorry?" Father MacTavish blinked.

"I divorced him three months ago." She let go of the lifeless hand. "I'm no longer Mrs. Boarden."

Father MacTavish nodded before walking out of the hospital room.

"Three years you hung on." She sniffed back a tear. "You had to drive. Get behind the wheel. Show you're the man."

The nurse shifts her weight a little, wanting to escape.

"I told you, stop drinking. But no, you had to be the man." Brenda reaches out and slaps her once husband's face. "You're an asshole. Our children… Now I have nothing. I hope you burn in hell."

DUNGON

I stare at the stone archway, trying to will the guards to come down and feed me. It's been three days, and my concave stomach aches with need. I'm ravenous to the point of feeding on the person who died yesterday, but already see someone has beaten me. My civilized mind is slipping with the pure need to survive.

We used to talk, all of us who are locked down here, and joke that it was all a bad dream. After so long, I would enjoy talking again. Is there still hope? I don't know anymore. Hope is something you feel inside. All I have is the emptiness of starvation. Even the old Wizard is stuck down here. Silver chains hold his power at bay. A chain made of precious metal is still a chain.

I'm pulled away from my daunting existence by the sound of metal clad feet hitting the stairs. Torchlight plays with shadows in the archway, casting ghoulish shapes against the wall. Shadows of gnashing teeth and long clawed hands come. The nightmares of a starving man bleeds into my reality. I want to scream, but my dry throat prevents anything but a mild croak.

Light shadows the guards entering our private little hell. I squint against the sudden pain the brightness brings. Our captors mumble in some language I'm not familiar with, and I cower into my little space against the wall as much as possible.

One of them steps toward the dead body and toes it, as if the dead could jump up and strangle him. The glint of metal shows from under the cloak he wears, and there's a greave protecting a shin just above the pointed sabaton. A few seconds pass. A scowl erupts from the guard, and it draws back a foot. A crunch echoes through the small room. I cringe. The guard turns to his companion and mutters something, who comes forward and performs the same test. Bones shatter under dead skin. One produces a key from behind his cloak and unlocks the shackles.

Two more guards step forward and hoist the body between them. Grunting, they cart the body away. Just three guards stay, each stepping between the grovelling mass of humanity. They pull back as hands reach out for any sign of kindness or relief. One even utters something and kicks out at the outstretched hand of a child.

We number thirty, and overpowering the three should be easy, but like the rest I cower against the stone wall, seeking protection from being noticed. I'm still not ready to give up my life.

A thud and crunch echoes in the cavernous depression of our home. A child wails.

"You didn't have to do that," a woman shouts. She clutches the child to her chest. "She's hungry, you heartless bastards! We need food! You haven't fed us in days!"

A stream of nonsensical words come out from behind the guard's cowl.

"Don't care! Starving here! Child cries for stomach. You prance swearing at—"

His gauntlet swings out and catches the woman in the face. Her head whips back. A snap fills the air. Her lifeless form falls over, crushing the child.

Hooded guards stand motionless. The body fails to move. How little our lives mean to them. I force myself even deeper into the joint of the wall and floor. There must be a way for me to escape.

The tableau is broken as one guard unshackles the woman. His gauntleted hand grasps her hair and pulls the body away. The child lays still and quiet. The other guard picks it up by a leg, holding the filthy body at arms-length, as if the death repelled some inner humanity.

Garbled speech bounces off the walls around us. The guards nod under their hoods and step around our cowering mass to exit the room whence they came. Boots scrape and clank as they ascend some hidden staircase.

A voice breaks the silence, "It could've been worse."

The whisper is gravelly, as if the throat had not been used for a long time. I glance around, startled by the eyes of the old man, slightly open and watery. Deep lines etch away from the corners of those eyes. Angry red hues where lids come together, and streaks of crimson decorate the whites. Those eyes hold me for a second, then I gather the strength to turn away.

"You are strong," the old man says. "Not many people can break from the gaze of a Wizard of my standing." A shuttering breath escapes his body. "Even in my weakened state."

"I'm already cursed, Wizard. Do not further my misfortune." I place one hand over my heart with fingers splayed and draw a squiggle with the index of the other, the way Mother taught me all those lifetimes ago to ward myself against evil.

"There is no worry for you," the Wizard wheezes. "Wizards do not curse people, only a Sorceress would do such evil things."

I hazard a glance at him. The Wizard is hunched up, eyes now closed from what I can tell with the limited lighting in the dungeon. Calmness comes over me knowing he is no longer watching. With a shaking hand, I reach out to gain a little more slack in the chains. His hand blurs, grabs the chain, and pulls before I can react. His grip is like steel on my wrist. I try to pull back. His strength is enough to kill.

"I intend to escape." The whisper is barely audible. He leans forward. "But I need your help."

I'm nothing special. A farmer always trying to grow one more cabbage to get something, anything, to make life more comfortable, but never able to keep ahead of the tax collector. It's part of the reason I'm a captive. He watches me with bent head, gazing from under bushy eyebrows that obscure the deep green of his eyes.

"I'm no one," I say, struggling to free my hand. "Let me go. Maybe someone else will help you."

He lifts a beard covered chin, the scrunch of skin between his eyes becoming less pronounced. He almost looks fatherly. "What caused you to become this way?" Even talking softly, his voice bounces like a cart on a loose-gravel road.

I turn my back on him, wishing I had spoken up like the woman with the child. At least the guards would have put me out of my misery.

"What is your name?" His chains clink with the slightest movement.

A scream wells up from my memory. Mother, standing to the side of a blazing fire, screaming at Father for telling his name to an old man he'd never before met. "I have no name."

"Everything has a name," the Wizard says. "Trees have names. I've spoken to many of them in my long life. The flies in the air have names, very long names, knowing their short lives. Ants have names, though only the flying ones seem to have male names. Even a small patch of moss has a name." His body shakes with coughing. "Even these"—he holds out his arms, shaking the chains—"have names. They are a bastardization of the Dragon tongue. Bestiliatolen, that is their name. Each glyph coloured with the blood of an Elven maiden killed on the full moon of her 170th birthday." His eyes gloss over. "I do so miss those maidens."

73

I listen, absorbing all he says about the young ladies. For a moment, I can see them in my mind and forget about the horrid existence I'm forced into. Those green eyes are less blood shot. A sheen of sweat forms on his brow, and he shivers. The story unveils, woven with a hypnotic rhetoric that pulls me in. He's trudging over a vast desert, creating water out of the air, saving hundreds from certain death. Next, he crosses into a desolate wasteland and creates food for starving masses. Children, stomachs distended, crowd around his legs, hands outstretched. The Wizard laughs and produces sweets for them in rolling waves of sugary delight.

It changes. Lights dim. Mildew enters the air. A dark cavern swallows us. We trudge downward. Shadows dance an eerie waltz on the walls. Heat washes the perspiration from his weary body as rocks, black as pitch, try desperately to trip tired feet. A great maw yawns before us, and glowing red streaks the stalactites overhead. Droplets of fire bounce off an invisible shield surrounding us.

My reflection stands next to the Wizard. His arm outstretched, holding a staff of petrified wood. In the head of the staff, a small purple jewel glows brighter than the sun. He utters unintelligible words. The dragon before us roars. Its scaled throat arches to the ceiling. One foot with claws longer than my body, crushes down on us, stopped by that dome of power.

A battle erupts. Wizard circling, chanting. Dragon circles, roaring. The Wizard tires in the battle, each spell he casts taking more of his strength. A bolt of lightning arcs from his outstretched fingers and hits the cavern ceiling. The shield around us crumbles in a shower of tinkling ice. It melts without leaving any water on the ground. But the Wizard smiles at the beast and points upward.

A smile lights the ends of the dragon's mouth, and then its head hits the ground. Blood, red and hot, pours from its mouth. The Wizard slumps and I catch him.

"It is good." Breath wheezes from his lungs. "I have slain the beast. The villages are safe."

The blunt end of thick stalactites now crowns the beast's head. We offer no glance back while ascending the long cavern to the open air.

I blink. Glance away from the hypnotic eyes. He did it again, captured me even more than before. I slide backward, away from the wheezing Wizard and make the sign of warding. He laughs.

"That would only hold back pixies and newts!" He coughs, rattling phlegm from deep in his lungs. "You must excuse me. Sharing thoughts takes much out of the body, and these flairs have kept me drugged since they captured me."

"If you have been drugged, how are you awake now?" Curiosity inched me forward.

The hairs in his beard move, centre lifting and edges falling. "I thought that would be obvious." He motions about. "They have not fed us in a long time. Longer than the last time they let us starve."

"They drug your food?"

"Yes," he replies. "Probably with crushed poppies or something like that. There was a time I liked to stuff my pipe with them." He stares off into the distance again.

"Then why are you eating it?"

He scowls and turns away from me. "When hunger takes you, and once drugged, you don't know better than to eat what is put in front of you."

The guards come back with food and water. When they approach the Wizard, one grabs his hair, yanking back the old head, while another shoves the gruel into the gapping mouth.

The Wizard's eyes glaze over as awareness slips from him. He is lost once again.

Time passes, for what else do we have but time now. A thought, that even with the meagre food we receive, I can still share my bowl with him, allowing the drug to leave his system. I've seen his memories. He's a powerful Wizard. I could escape with him. We could all escape with him. If we tried, together, sharing just a little food each to allow him to regain his composure.

I'll talk with the others.

The guards drop food off after two more days. One motions to the Wizard, but the other shakes his head. The bowl is left at his side, and they leave.

I inch closer to the Wizard and stop his hand from shoveling in the food. He drools and struggles to break my restraining grip.

"Here, take this." I shove my bowl into his hands, and he eats mechanically. I can go another few days without eating. It will be someone else's turn next time.

The guards feed us again, and it's only been a day. I nod to a blond man with one eye to exchange his food with the Wizard. He shakes his head and dips into the bowl. My face reddens as I motion again with a shaking hand. A large man, with the scars of sword fighting on his body, but now wasted away to just a heavy sack of flesh, cuffs him upside the head. A howl, and the untainted bowl slides across the floor toward me. I hand it off to the Wizard and slide the bad food back. The blond one takes it and eats. Soon, he is in a slumber. Thoughts of choking him in his sleep creep through my mind.

I examine the Wizard closely, holding open one eye and trying to see the man who was there only a few days ago, but nothing looks back at me. Some things take time, I remind myself.

Sleep fights its way to me through the dirty floor, and my belly full after two days of eating, I release myself to its gentle escape.

Humanity can be a cruel joke. We eat, sleep, defecate, and survive. Our bathroom is a chain length away from where we sleep. But not much comes out except a small splash and turd. My arms, once strong and thick, now are but twigs of small branches attached to my torso. And my body, once muscular and strong from farming, is now concaved upon itself. I wonder how many months, if not years, it will take to be a working man again. That is if I get out of here and survive the escape.

The blond man hasn't woken up yet. The guards dropped food off and another gave up their rations for the Wizard. He needs to wake, to show us we can escape somehow. I don't know how long the group will keep feeding him.

His eyes roll a little. Not much, but something tells me he will rouse soon. Maybe there is salvation yet.

The guards fed us again this morning, and the Wizard woke. His eyes foggy with sleep and head wobbly, but now I can show the others he can help us out.

"Are you well?"

"Umph... Sore... Water..."

My cup and bowl have enough water to wet his lips. I bring it over, drop what I can on his lips, and ease him down. "That's all there is until the guards come back."

"How… Long?" The effort of speaking is taking its toll on him.

"Only a stretch of days, six at the most. Now stay still and pretend to be drugged for the guards."

He slips into a deep sleep, eyes rolling back in their sockets.

The Wizard holds out his arms again, shackles gleaming in the failing light. "I have gained a lot of my strength back, thanks to you."

His praise goes out to all of us, and he gazes at each one.

"Someone has to help get us out," I say. "How much longer?"

He crunches his lips together, brow making one caterpillar above his eyes. "One more meal ought to do it." He points to some rubble. "You there, blacksmith, right?"

A man who towers over all of us with skin flaps decorating his body, nods.

"There is a rock there that appears to be orthoclase feldspar. Could you toss it over here?"

The man tosses over the rock, and I quickly snatch it before the small thing hits the Wizard. I turn the rock over, looking at it from different sides. The pale pink-brown colour and knobby corners seem hard but blunt. I glance up, and the Wizard is staring at me.

"Since you have the rock, might as well put it to good use." He thrusts out his arms. "Start blemishing the writing."

It takes me several days of hammering, but the characters on the Wizard's manacles are all marred beyond recognition. A sense of pride in a job well done flows through my body, and the old man grins.

"One more thing to do. It's luck that silver is the only metal able to bind my powers. Come here with that rock."

He pulls his old body to a fallen brick on the ground and places his manacled hand upon it. "You need to break the manacle for me to be able to cast. Once broken, I can free my other hand, and then everyone here."

"How did they capture you?" I had never asked this, but a desire to know tells me it's important now. The need to know is overpowering.

"They snuck up on me."

"But how? The guards wear noisy armour and walk with heavy strides."

"It's of no consequences now! Hurry, hit the chains and get me free!" His eyes burn with the power of conviction.

I remember something similar the day they pulled me from my small farm. The tax man, saying I owed so much to the Count, ordered my farm sold in order to collect. The guards marching in, taking me from my home, and the fire, oh that fire, burning down the hut I built. So many months of labour, destroyed with a small torch. It wasn't much, but it was mine. And now I have nothing. Not even my freedom.

The rock falls against the bindings, offering a clink as it hits, forcing a shock through my arms. I tried it prior only to find the marking protected them sending lightning through my hands and up my arms.

"Again!" the Wizard says.

"Tell me how." I raise the rock.

"It was the time of reaping. I was busy saving a town when someone snuck up and wrapped me in a silver chain." His stare bore into me. "There was nothing I could do. Once my power was shackled, I was defeated."

The rock comes down and clinks against the shackle's binding. My fingers cry with pain. "But how?"

I raise the rock, waiting for his response. My teeth gritted against the anticipated shock.

"There are a lot of things in this world that work against us." He motions to the others who watch in the background. None of them offered to help. "It took the blacksmith a leap of faith to toss the rock to you. Each has their own chains to escape from. Their own demons. Devils." He takes a deep breath. "Even I have my own fears. Things that make me pause when fighting the evil around us."

The rock comes down and clanks again.

"Tell me about your fears, Wizard." I raise the rock again, wondering how many times I will have to bash it to remove the bindings. How long will my aching arm hold out? Will my fingers keep their grasp on the rock?

"I fear growing old." His voice is soft, only loud enough for me to hear. "I have walked this land for many years. More than you could imagine. Seen many things."

The rock clanks against the shackles.

"I've travelled from the mountain of Tripellie to the boarders of the Southern Wasteland. Each time seeing too many people suffer. Children praying for food that never comes, parents wondering how they would survive. I've battled men, women, the barbarians of the north, the headsman of the south."

I lift the rock again, waiting for him to finish.

"The world is changing while we are locked up here."

I bring the rock down. It smacks against the shackle, the thunk more solid than the last.

"Time is nothing but infinite, when there is no way to measure it."

I lift the rock.

"We live, we die."

I bring the rock down.

"And nothing changes."

The rock is raised again.

"All we can do is ride the carriage."

Down comes the rock.

"And hope that no one kicks us off."

Up goes the rock.

"The only thing worth living for is freedom."

Down comes the rock.

"And the chance to be with a good woman."

Up comes the rock.

He stares into my eyes, a wanting hides behind them. Something is telling me not to free this monster on the world, to hold back. Take the isolation. Remain a prisoner of the unknown, the Flairs as the Wizard calls them. Never again to experience the touch of a woman. But then I find myself full of desire for the wide open plains of my homeland. To run my fingers through newly tilled soil. I desire to live off the land as I once had done.

The rock comes down.

A shackle splits.

He is free.

The Wizard stares at the chains as they fall, clinking into a small pile at his feet. He wastes no time. A wave of his gnarled hand turns my chains to dust. I glance around, and everyone is examining their wrists, and the lack of chains around them.

Free. We are all free.

Energy fills my limbs at the realization. We now must escape.

The Wizard grins at me and nods.

I stand, and several others stand a well. A glimpse toward the stairs brings a hand on my arm.

"Not that way," the Wizard says, his voice stronger now. "We're not using the stairs."

With sure steps, the Wizard approaches the wall. People step aside, others cower away. He picks up a rock, scraps it against the wall in a circle. Strange mutterings come out of him, and finally he throws the rock against the circle. Instead of bouncing off the wall, it travels through, taking the stacked stones with it. We have a tunnel, and light is at the end.

We run until our legs burn and can carry us no farther. It does not take long, but with the cavern far behind us, my spirit is alit. Very few follow us out of the dungeon.

Exhausted, we collapse at the bank of a river, drinking until we are near sick. It is the first time I feel no thirst.

Twenty of us followed the Wizard out of the dungeon and into freedom. Twenty hungry souls, looking for help to rebuild their existence. We all look toward our saviour, wanting, waiting, expecting to hear something that will set us free of the unknown.

"I need to rest," he says, hungry gaze flittering about those who followed. "And the warmth of someone."

I muster up the energy to scratch my head. A glance at other members of our group shows them as confused. I step forward. "What do you mean?"

"You," he says, pointing at a young woman. "Come to me, child."

A girl, no older than sixteen, steps forward. Her blank eyes and matted brown hair belie a beauty of youth. She moves mechanically, as if someone controls her. The Wizard moves his hands, small droplets of sweat forming on his brow.

"Be with me tonight. Refresh my soul." The smile upon his face is crocked. And as she walks forward I know there's a problem. We are sacrificing the bindings of one captor for another, and that is not escaping. It is servitude to those who repress. The images from his mind fall apart, and I see them for what they are. Pure fiction.

A rock is placed in my hand, the very one used to free us. I balance it, playing upon the skills taught to me by my father when hunting rabbits in the field. My arm goes back, then hurtles forward.

The strike hits the Wizard in the forehead, and he topples backward like an oak tree falling to the woodsman's axe. The uncertainty and worry that gripped me through the escape lifts. The girl blinks, then stumbles backward, escaping the mesmerizing force. She is free, and the last chain that bound us is broken.

80

2084

I have to believe there is more to life than this drivel of an existence, but there it is before me, the document, a strip of plastic, outlining another five year contract. The fake paper lies on a fake wood desk, with fake leather chairs around it, and fake fresh air blasting through the building. No real scent permeates the air, just chemicals used to give euphoria, so when they present the contract, you sign thinking it is the best. But each year they claw back a little more, build you up a little less, and demand so much more of you.

This year, I will take a stand.

Slowly, I place a finger on the edge, careful not to touch the spot to record my fingerprint. No need to make the system think I'm accepting the new contract. The temperature changes from comfortably warm to chill in seconds. Anxiety starts to crawl up my spine as the chemicals switch to induce fear of the unknown. The whispers of subliminal messages float in the air. The wall screen flickers a little, signalling a switch in the program. I hate that this happens in my home, but when the workers appeared ten years ago and installed the system control, there was nothing that could be done to stop them. I signed that contract. I put my life in their hands. I brought it upon myself.

It's not like there's a choice. Everyone goes through the same thing. Now, with the world heading into destruction, all we have are three corporations to work for, but most of us believe they're the same one. Pick one, sign a five year contract, renew it, and work until you die.

The alternative, go off grid, become an outlaw, steal food and power.

I like my freedom, if you can call it such. Time to exercise what can only be called disobedience. Why they ask us to sign contracts is beyond me. They own the courts and lawyers. They own the politicians. They own everything.

The paper shimmers, updates, flashes. I've never seen it do such. This is the first time I've rejected their proposal, so I'm not sure what to expect. Tentatively, I reach out and turn the page toward me. My eyes water after a second of scanning. They changed the chemicals again. It's hard to focus. I pull out a tissue and wipe my eyes. After a few seconds, the tears recede, and all the glory of updates show highlighted. They reduced my signing bonus.

I stand, not bothering to turn the paper back to the system, and walk out the door of my office. This is it, the end of two decades.

My cell rings. Corporate is calling. I swipe *ignore*. Another ring, now on the net line. I'm confused, having never told them that number. The display shows "Private Number."

What can I do? For several seconds, I stare at the contract. The system cuts off and goes to the old answering machine I salvaged to screen calls. A busy signal erupts, and then the line drops. Strange.

I walk out of my office and into the living room, pick up the remote, and sit down on the couch. The ON button beckons me. It's the middle of the day, and everyone is working. When nothing is on worth watching, you need to use your streaming credits. The company will see it in the report, but I'm still on contract for another three days. I can't risk it.

The radio. It's on in a flash. Soothing music, the only true form of entertainment left to us, fills the room. I close my eyes and dream of a world without the pressures of today.

I drift off into blissful sleep as the subliminal messages enter from some corporate building to my home, and eventually into my subconscious.

Bright lights shine in my face, waking me up from a deep sleep. Three spots hover over me, and I wince at the brightness. How long was I out? The room is dark except for the three lights. It must be the middle of the night. Pain lances across my cheek as a sharp clap fills the air.

"Paul Seventeen, you didn't return to work," says a gruff man's voice.

I blink, rub my eyes to get the sleep out and wake up my brain. Another slap and searing pain.

"Paul Seventeen, you didn't return to work. You've violated your contract."

I sit up, shield my eyes from the light, but both hands come up. Something holds my wrists together. "Who–"

"Paul Seventeen, you have to wake up. Your response is needed on the contract."

Something shoves the plastic fake paper into my hands. It scrolls through the five year work agreement and stops at a section for my thumb print and voice signature.

"I'm not signing anything."

Pain erupts, but this time it's not my cheek, but stomach. I double over, try to hug my knees and guard myself at the same time.

The wafting sound of a plastic paper fills the air. "Finger print and sign."

I lift my head. "I told you, I'm not sign–"

A blow lands on my cheek. It's not a light slap, but a fist. I fall sideways in a crouched position. Cold, hard, cement stops me. Blood collects on the floor from my mouth. I spit, and a tooth joins the pooling fluid.

"You were saying, citizen?" A heavy boot touches down beside my left hand. The plastic page drops on the floor. "We'll return in a few minutes to discuss this further."

Time is one of those ever-present details you can never escape. Mostly, we don't have enough of it, but other rare events give you too much. This is one of the too much moments.

I stare at the piece of plastic, wondering if I can find anything special about the contract now. It seems like the standard with all the special changes they did to it, but something also looks different—it is for only six months.

No one is employed for only six months. A year, maybe when they are just starting, but six months means you are terminally ill and not expected to survive past the seventh month. They want to have your employment terminated before you have any special need for benefits. Anything to reduce the bottom line.

A door opens and closes. Light footfalls echo in the room, and a pair of small white shoes stop in front of me. I look up. Her colourless uniform is a stark contrast to my red-stained one. She has the blank stare of someone who's seen it all and written a book about it, but something in the green eyes tells me to hold on. The woman keels down and holds out a cup with three capsules the size of horse pills, ends

83

black and green. A small curl of blonde hair peeks out of her cap to offset her eyes.

"You'll need your dose." Her eyes never waver as they bite into me. "I have some water as well."

I take the pill cup from her, hear the clunk of the large capsules against the plastic, and start to throw it away. Her hand comes out and stops me. "Take the pills."

A voice in the back of my head tells me to do as she says, but I don't know her. I pop one of the pills into my mouth, and bite down on it. The powder should explode and cause retching, but all I get is a sweet taste. I look up at her, eyes wide.

She nods, a small lift to the right corner of her mouth. "Take the pills."

I swallow the one in my mouth, then pop the other two. The water is placed in my other hand, and I chase the pills with it.

"Good. The pills will slow you down." She shakes her head. "Make you more manageable for the guards." She shakes her head again. "You will listen to them, and do as you're told." She nods this time. I get the message.

"Your name?" My voice is but a whisper.

"Martha Twenty-two." She stands, waits a second, then walks the way she came in.

"Martha?" I whisper.

"Yes, Paul Seventeen. We'll see each other again." A door opens and closes, leaving me in silence.

I lay on the floor, heat leaching from my body into the concrete. Blood no longer leaks from my mouth. The little pills Martha gave me are working wonders. I'm full, energized, awake. Something is very wrong. The pills usually put people into a docile mood, pull sheers before the eyes, take away desire. Generally, turns us into sheep.

Everything appears normal. Even the pain of the beating has subsided.

The door opens and closes. Feet stomp through the room and stop just before me. I don't move. Show no fear, but also pretend to be oblivious. This is the message I remember from years ago.

"Paul Seventeen, I see you haven't signed yet." A boot almost steps into the puddle of blood. "God, this guy's out of it."

"Get his print on the contract, maybe he'll sign once he sees it," another voice behind me replies.

It is my cue. Do something, but not much. Make them think the pills hit hard. I stir, lift my head a little and gaze out of slitted eyes. "You want me to sign something?" My voice slurs together, giving them the illusion I'm out of it.

Big Boots kneels down, pushes the plastic toward me. "Right there." His gloved finger touches the contract at the signature line.

I reach out, making a grand gesture, miss the line, and try again. My signature scrawls across the contract.

He stands, taking the contract with him.

"He signed already?" the second voice asks.

"Yeah, right where he should have. In blood no less."

"Give him the shot. We'll get him back to his home and collect a fast completion bonus."

A jab hits my arm. A little bee sting. All goes black.

I roll over in bed, open crusty eyes, and the room slowly lights up. The wall displays a news program and all is bad. Prices are going up. Taxes are going up. Unemployment is going up. Income is going down. They're increasing income tax to offset the latest economic numbers. We're to increase the number of times we visit the confession booths. I shake my head.

It's been four days since I signed the contract. Each day I take my pills. Each day I bite into one to see what is in it. Each day a sweetness erupts in my mouth. I believe Martha is taking care of me. The fog is lifting from my mind, and I can see clearly what our world is like.

I believed my home to be a palace of modern technology with every creature comfort. Looking at it now, I see four cramped rooms adjoining each other with a common centre. The kitchen sits to the North with nothing more than bland cubes for food. Thankfully, the pills supply me with enough energy. I tried one of the cubes and gaged at the taste.

I work, but it's getting hard. The tediousness of staring at the numbers to find the anomalies causes headaches. All I want is to close my eyes and ignore the screen. Nothing is the same as it was before I rebelled. Even the shows on my screen during rest period are repetitive drones of actors reading lines from pages they carry, nothing with any heart of feeling like before. My world has changed.

A knock spurs me into action. I get up, pull on my clothes, and head to the door.

One glance through the peep hole shows a person outside, big hat, tall, slender, wispy blonde hair. Someone I'm not familiar with. I hit the intercom. "Hello?"

"Paul Seventeen?"

The voice is familiar, so I open the door.

Martha pushes past me, and I get a bleak reminder of what it is like outside. The white hallway looks nothing like I remember. Everything is antiseptic. She takes off her hat, letting long hair tumble out and down her back. One of her fingers touches her lips and she starts to examine the room.

"I didn't know—"

She puts a finger to my lips, another on hers. I nod.

Martha spends ten minutes hunting around my home, looking for something without speaking. I follow her. She's under the bed, feeling around corners, opening drawers. Nothing is left unturned. She finishes and lets out a breath.

"We're clear." She slumps onto my couch, places her head in a hand.

"Clear of what?" I sit down beside her.

"No listening devices."

An ice cube runs up my back. "I ... what ... A listening device?"

She nods, sits up and reaches into a pocket. "They usually have them in most homes, but because you've renewed for six months they probably decided it's not worth it." A small electronic device drops from her hand onto the table. Its shinny surface is covered by scorch marks. "They look like that, but not as burnt."

"And what would have happened if you found one?" I pick up the device.

"Probably destroy it and leave it behind." She glances around. "Do you have any water?"

"Sure." I get up and go to the kitchen, grab a glass, and fill it. "How many have you found?"

"How many what?"

"Listening devices."

"Just that one."

I return with the water. "So, how did you know what to look for?"

She stares at me for a few moments. "Henry Five came to me while I disputed my contract." She takes the water and places it on the table. "He gave me the pills and the veil lifted from my eyes. It took about a week for my mind to clear up. I surmise you stopped taking the regular pills long before I did."

"You mean the supplements? Yeah, stopped taking them a few days before my contract expired."

"Why?"

I scratch my head. Why did I stop taking the supplements? That is a good question. It just happened. One day they just didn't find their way into my mouth, and that was it. "I don't know."

"I do." She picked up the glass and took a little sip, nodded, and put it down. "Your water is not being treated."

My brow furrows.

"Let me explain." Martha stands and walks to my kitchen. I stand and follow. "Water is supplied by the corporations. They feed and clothe us." She opens the cabinet under the sink. "Water comes in from the main piping station to your apartment and enters somewhere around here." She points to the pipes under the sink. "Each corp. supplies the chemicals to entice you to take the pills based on the subliminals. You stopped getting chemicals in the water and heard the subminals, thus went off the pills. Kind'a like what happened to me."

I nod.

"Henry explained it to me. The water makes you susceptible to subliminal suggestions, the suggestions make you take the pills, and then you are controlled." She stands and places hands on hips. "You come off a contract when something happens, like a disruption of the water, and you stop taking the pills. Once off the pills, you start questioning things. Don't sign a contract, refuse orders, go out more. Stuff like that."

"I was getting a little antsy sitting around the house."

"I figured that." She takes another look around. "Not much of a furniture person, are you?"

"Use what works." I motioned back to the living room.

We walk into the room, and Martha sits on the couch again. "The world is not as it seems." She tosses me a small flash drive. "This will explain it better. Disconnect your screen from the network before starting it, though."

I look at the drive. Written across the small surface are the numbers 2018. Curiosity gets me. I walk over to the screen, reach behind, and pull the network connection before turning it on. The drive goes into the reader, and the file menu appears. I tap the only file.

Vibrant colours fill the screen. Green, blue, yellow. They twirl around and coalesce into a dot. I blink. Skin tingles. The dot then explodes into millions of dots, and they expand on the screen, leaving behind four numbers, 2084. The numbers pulse with a deepening crimson before fading. Numbers, letters, and symbols start to scroll up from the lower screen. A narrative begins.

Awe builds up inside me, quickly turns to concern, then my cheeks heat up. The narrative voice has a calming quality about it.

"Our world is controlled by the corporations. They tax, they make us work, they control us. We have no free will, no recourse, no way out."

The narrator, voice a little gruff, tells of how the world used to be years ago. "We lived in homes dotting the countryside with children and multi-generational households. The joy people felt by putting in an honest day to come home to a meal, not of cubes, but of real food. Raising children filled me with pride. But then came the rise of the corporations, and the fall of government."

The screen changed. Large towers grew, thrusting into the sky. A tear runs down my face as darkness descends, and the outline of a business-suited man shows and he grows horns. Evil, that is the message.

"The corporations enslaved us, like man did to everyone at one time or another throughout history. And the once happy people, who worked thirty to forty years and then retired with pensions to live out the rest of their lives in comfort, soon found themselves on contracts, swapped from one corporation to another. Never to retire, only work until their hearts give out or brains turn soft."

"We have lost ourselves," I say as another tear traces a line down my cheek.

The screen morphs into a large box with two spinning wheels on its face. Once again the narrator changes his focus. "Then the computers took over, replacing the men who were in charge of the corporations. They run things more efficiently, and all of mankind becomes enslaved. Chemicals and subliminal messages are the controlling method used, for they are cheap and easy to produce. People, enslaved by the corporate machines, found no recourse but to keep working until they died."

My heart falls. No way about it, we are slaves. Even being free of the control, I am still a slave. And the message becomes more disturbing. People not susceptible to the drugs or conditioning, found themselves on short-term contracts. Food no longer supplied. Water stopped. Existence terminated. Retirement through death.

I hung my head, shaking it in disbelief.

Martha takes my hand and gives it a squeeze. I turn to her, and she points to the screen. "It's not finished."

"But we can rise up against the machines. Time will roll by, and we can finally succeed by destroying the machines." The screen shows people swing bats. The machines crumble into parts. A message scrolls across, "This could be our reality."

I reach over and take the drive out of the screen. "I knew something was controlling us, but didn't know what."

"Not everyone is aware." Martha sits on the couch. "It's very rare that someone gets free of the drugs and is able to survive."

This startles me. "Able to survive?"

Martha nods. "Usually, a freed person rebels so hard that the system catches them. I was near the end of my contract, so were you. We are lucky."

I scan the small rooms that, at one time, appeared extravagant to my foggy mind. "You call this lavish?"

"I call it surviving." Martha reached for the water. "Besides, now that you are free, there's no limit to what can be done. There are three of us now, that I know of."

Only three. I'm concerned about the numbers. "How can three people effect change?"

Martha chuckles. "I know three. You, Henry, and me. Henry knows three, me, himself, and the one who freed him. There is a line that goes on. Henry told me the one who freed him knows a lot more, for he freed more than just Henry. You're my first."

We talked for hours. Martha found herself pulled into the duties of a nurse early in life. Not that she liked it, but the corporations believed it suited her.

Like me, she wanted to explore. But our sedentary life under the company's control did little to allow us such. Ten hour days, four hours relax, eight hours sleep. In there we needed to find enough time to visit a confessional. The strange booths sat everywhere in the compound.

I looked at my watch—I'm late for my next session.

"I have to go." Without waiting for Martha to reply, I stand and walk to the door. "You can stay if you like, I need to have the confessional, or my current contract is voided."

"I'll wait." Martha picks up the remote. "I find it interesting what we used to believe was entertainment."

I nod, she is no longer looking at me. Why do I feel indifferent?

Out the door and down the long corridor I go. It used to appear so sparse and open, but now it's just crowded, smelly, and dank. After a few minutes of walking I come across a confessional with no line, but someone is inside. I wait.

Three minutes pass, then five. Foreboding makes me want to find another booth, but I know if I leave this one, it will become vacant. Others walk past, their glances empty, unfocused, as if they can see through me.

Ten minutes and the door opens. A tall man, face familiar, exits while popping pills into his mouth. I hesitate for only a second, then enter.

The doors close, leaving total darkness and silence. A light blinks to my left and I place a palm on it. A prick touches my middle finger. I never noticed it before, but it explains the callus on that finger. The screen before me comes to life. A soft glow that brightens into the face of a non-descript man.

"How are you, brother?"

I stare at the image, reach out, and touch the smooth surface.

"You seem distracted, brother."

"I … I was told to come." There, I've blurted it out.

"If you were told to come, then it must have been a long time since your last confession."

I wait a few seconds before answering. Is there a reason to lie? The confessional is something we all do and it takes care of us, or so I remember. "Yes, a long time. Almost five days."

"That is a long time. Tell me, what troubles you?"

Something entices me to speak, so I do. Everything comes out. The contract, the beating, the pills. I talk about the contract, about what Martha told me, how she slipped me the new pills. Then the truth about the water comes out, the difference it made in my life.

Like always, the confessional listens intently. Nothing makes it sway of change. We have a link. A shared companionship beyond that which mere man and machine usually have. And when done, I sit there and cry. My body heaves while attempting to suck in breath. A sweet scent of lilacs fills the confessional, and tranquility starts to come over me. Then cinnamon drifts in the air, making me settle into an easy rhythm of breathing.

I swear the face is smiling, but with just eyes and mouth showing it is hard to truly tell.

"Are you fully confessed, brother?"

A deep breath shudders through me. "Yes … Yes, I believe I am."

The scent changes to one of oranges, and four pills drop out of the dispenser. Apples float in the air with the oranges, and a small cup drops into view. Water dispenses into the cup. I reach out.

"You must be thirsty. Drink."

I take the cup and drink.

"For your health. One pill."

I take a pill, put it in my mouth, and swallow with more water. It is reflexive. Something that I have done all my life as far back as my memory can go. Like breathing, the motion is something unconscious, driven by the mind.

"Is there anything you would like to say, Paul Seventeen?"

My mind reels with a euphoria I've never felt before. The confessional bursts with colours and scents. A wonderful kaleidoscope of enjoyment not seen for ages. Like a man wandering the desert, I drink it in with my senses as if it were water. Even the image outlined on the monitor is sharper, full of vibrant life. A smile arches on the face, one of kindness and love.

"You are ready to go now. Be in peace, brother."

The image fades, and the door opens. I find myself walking in an open field of green grass. Trees line down either side of the field, and birds fly through the air. I gape at the sight, wondering why it was absent for so long.

Work, I must get to work. If I don't, there will be no time to enjoy this later. Not stopping to talk to a person, I rush home to my lavish bungalow.

The door is open, a mess of papers on the floor. I pick them up. They go into the recycling box, ready for disposal by the curb. The maid is there, moving about in his black uniform and waving a duster about. Its fluffy top still black from all the dust it must have picked up. I smile, thank him for cleaning up the mess and he grins in gratitude.

A large bag is near a new couch, the old one partially out the door. I smell sulfur in the air and the room sparkles from a recent washing.

"Is it spring already?" I ask.

He stops, black boots dotted with red. "Yes, it is spring, brother."

"You must have washed the rug and couch. Was there a problem?"

Another smile. "My brother spilled something on the couch." He waves at the other maid pushing the couch out the door. "We replaced it for you."

"Thank you. Very kind." I see the black bag on the floor. It is long, skinny, and there are a few strands of blonde hair sticking out. "Did you

91

find lots of dirt?" I point at the bag.

"A really big ball of it, brother. A really big ball."

He hoists the bag on one shoulder, starts for the door. "If you need us, just call out and we'll come running."

"Thank you."

"You're welcome, brother."

FLASH FICTION

Rocket Boy

Bravery comes in many forms, from the men on the battlefield to the pilot in the sky. I know this to be true. Many would say we are warmongers, only in it for the kill. But that is not true. From the time I strapped on the pack, I knew I would fly high and never fear those below me.

All is ready.

Months of testing, years of dreaming. Soon, I will show it was not in vain. Even the clothes covering my body are special, picked out by two assistants just days before. Each piece tailored meticulously, ready to protect me from harm.

Checking my helmet, dirty fingers slide the goggles in place, offering protection. On the top of the roof, one foot moving forward, I take to the air in my jet pack, knowing the fuse is lit.

Words

Tara pulled the cart, trying to ignore Joshua as he jumped into every puddle singing that damn song over and over again.

"It's raining, it's pouring, the old man is snoring …"

"Enough, Joshua." She glanced about the market square, wondering if the rain would ever stop. Another torn page from a newspaper wafted in the wind, drenched but the print still legible. "Grab that and put it in the cart."

Joshua dashed out from beside her and took hold of the page. "What is it?"

"Fuel." She pulled her tattered coat tighter. The rain picked that time to intensify its desire to make her miserable. It succeeded.

"Why?" Joshua placed the paper in the cart. He stared at the small print in wonderment.

"It'll be cold tonight, and if we want to be warm, we need it." Her gaze drifted to the stalls of people putting away food from the afternoon market. A grumble roared in her stomach. "This is a dreadful planet."

"Why don't we leave?"

For what appeared to be the thousandth time for her, she pondered the same thing. Why did they stay here? Nothing was keeping them, besides the need to convert what they could into fuel for the ship. At this rate, it would take another five years.

"The people here hoard words." She pointed at another page. "There!"

Joshua darted out to secure the fuel base, and Tara, seeing the merchant turn his back, took one of the last books from his table and held it tight. Her mind spun. Was there enough here to break down into fuel? Enough to escape? No, but it could supply enough if they just found a few more sheets.

"Mother!" Joshua stared at her, the page clutched in his grimy hand.

Tara blushed, her voice just a whisper. "Desperate times." She turned her gaze to him from under sharp eyebrows. "Now run!"

She shoved the book under her coat, grabbed the cart, and then ran toward the forest edge. Hate for what she did filled her.

"Stop! Thief!" came the voice of a man behind them.

The sound of chairs overturning reached her. Men from the market gave chase, following them from forgotten stalls, but too slowly. Tara manoeuvred them into the underbrush. The stream would stop the pursuers, but not Josh and her. She motioned to Joshua.

Her son drew out a small bar and it expanded. The pole end dug into the ground and propelled him over the rushing water to the other side.

"Catch!" She threw the cart and took out her own bar, hoping there was enough power left in it.

The swift rush of air pushed her from the ground, and she landed beside Joshua. "We may just make it now."

"Are the words enough?" Joshua rummaged through her mother's coat and came out with the book.

"Let me see it." She grabbed the book and opened it. Pictures. Tara cried.

"What is it, Mother? Are there enough words to power our craft or what?"

Tara could not answer. Tears brimmed her eyes. She closed them and dropped the book. Frustration welled inside her.

Joshua picked it up and started to cry as well.

"We have to find another market. Maybe we can get more words from the blowing wind." Joshua turned his face up and looked into Tara's eyes.

"We are lost." Tara's shoulders slumped. "The engine cannot take us anywhere else. We needed words, and all we got was this!" She wanted to burn it, burry it, destroy every page, but instead, waved her hand at the offensive material her son carried.

"But there are lines on it. Can we not use them?"

"You are too young to understand," Tara replied. "The engine is powered by the words of imagination. This book ... this beautiful collection of pages, would have been enough if only ..."

Joshua dropped the book and took his mother's hand. She saw realization in his eyes, even without knowing what it actually was.

Words. They needed words for the engine to run, but this book had no words. The pages turned and the two stared at the lines. At the top, in a language neither of them understood, the words stood out for them to see. *For ages 2-5, colour inside the lines.*

A Cold Evening

The stars are different here. Ursa Minor to the north and the big dipper, are inverted. Who could believe the surface could be such a drastic contrast from day to night? With the suns down, condensation turns to frost, and a bluish snow drops from the sky. I check the outside temperature.

"-30 and dropping." I pull the sleeping bag up higher.

Sheila cuddles up. A shock from her cold feet against my shin runs through me. "You wanted to go camping. Bill said this was the best planet for the whole experience."

"Yes, it is, I guess. Twin suns orbiting at a distance. Did you turn on the oxygen exchange?"

"Sure did."

I nod. The atmosphere will become liquid with both the suns down. When they set, the experiment will begin.

"What's in the soup can?" She snuggles into me, nosing my neck.

"That's the question. I told Bill to surprise us. The only thing is he had to take the label off, and it had to be okay to either heat up or freeze." I glance at the thermometer, -60.

"How long before the air goes liquid?"

"Not sure, but the way the temp is dropping, I'd guess not too much longer. I'll open the roof once it is. The atmospheric phenomenon should start at that time." I kiss the top of her head. Ten years to get here, and thousands of light years away from Earth. Hope she's enjoying this trip.

Sheila wiggles a little closer. "Did you clean up the containers?"

"Damn, that's what I forgot." I start to disentangle from her.

"No, don't worry."

"They warned us about cleaning up. Something we have to do after every meal."

"Who will know?"

I stop struggling, who would know? It's not like there's some crazy animal on this planet that'd eat frozen Chinese food.

"Is it time?"

I look, -330. "Yes, it's time."

A press of the remote and the roof becomes transparent.

"What about the walls? Can we do them as well? I really want to see the landscape now that it's not being broiled by the day."

With a small adjustment, I clear the walls. We both stare as the deep blue mountains rise in the background. The now liquefied atmosphere rolls around like thick fog. A small figure of a man sniffs at the Styrofoam containers of Chinese food. He holds up the pale crescent of the cookie, smiling, and pulls the paper out discarding the rest. Even an alien knows better than to eat a fortune cookie.

One Last Time

Marge sits in the chair, eyes heavy, while strangers walk past. Respectfully, they offer their condolences and press her hand between theirs. She nods and smiles, thanking them for coming.

Floral bouquets add colour to the bleak room. She remembers a time when David gave her one every day, and a dozen on Valentine's Day. Those were the days when their hearts danced at the mere mention of each other's name. She caresses the smooth laminated wood next to her, and a smile graces her lips.

He would have liked to see the many who came out today.

Father Benjamin arranged everything. David said the man was a stuffed shirt at the best of times, but he did care. So, she left everything up to him. The priest even refused the money she wanted to donate, saying her long-time attendance was more than enough. She still slipped the bills into the poor box. David would have liked that.

Six young men stand to the side of the room, waiting to give honours to David one last time. The tall man holds a lambskin apron and a sprig of acacia. They speak from a book, place the sprigs in his coffin, and point to the sky. Marge smiles, and wonders who they are and how they knew her husband. A large rotund man stands at the podium, giving some words about how fleeting life is, and how the loss of one affects all. His tuxedo is too tight across the back and middle.

David lost so much weight in the end. She had fussed for hours trying to get it just right for him, only to see it bunched up. Her want to make it perfect took over. She knew it needed taking in, but pins would work just fine now. Her fingers ached while pinning the right places, but she fixed it just right.

The man finishes talking and places a small piece of evergreen beside

David. An attendant touches Marge's arm, guiding her to say goodbye one last time. This is what she'd worried about. No longer seeing his kind face after today.

When they first met, it was passion that ruled their lives. Then, as newlyweds, they could hardly keep their hands off one another. Lust blossomed into love, and they held each other's hand, even when anger interrupted their relationship. When their bodies started to fail, he still insisted they share the same bed. She knew he still loved her even though he could not express it physically. He shared his bed with no other. For this she was certain.

A tear traces a line down her cheek as she caresses his face for the last time. And even though he is lost to this world, he is not lost to her heart. She will always love her David. She will always love her valentine.

Power

There is an ache as I reach out a skeleton-like hand toward my thick-lensed glasses. Nothing pains me more than this time of day. It's the hour when an orange sun starts its journey to the horizon. A question runs through my mind, will this be the last time I can see?

Ignore the pain in my joints is all I can do. The years are not kind, but denying death is the only joy left in life. Not even the warmth of a fur coat can bring my bones back from the icy grip that a lack of circulation affords me. No, I will beat off death with my cane if needed.

With creaking knees, I push myself up and allow the last dwindling light to strike a hand. One small spot smokes before the orb of death shrinks down. The heating pad drops to the side and no longer works. Desperation clutches inside, working uncaring fingers against a heart no longer pumping for the joy of life.

One light flickers to life, then another. The small room, filled with dirt and decay welcomes my frown. Gray hair, short and mussed from the sleep of the dead, clutches against a skull no longer able to support its growth. But one day, the cure will be found.

Now there is still the need to get up and feed. One more night. One more chance. One more victim.

The last of the heat escapes the covers as I whip them away. Strength is failing, but I have enough to lift an absurdly light frame out of the coffin. A little wobble, but nothing that cannot be fixed with nourishment.

More lights blink into existence as the cave comes to life. It is a mockery of my existence. The place shows more and more how much the change has taken away from me.

Another century, perhaps? Maybe, but who can tell the passage of time with nothing to mark it but the setting sun. And what year is it? Last I remember was 1872.

The roaring of the small town of York, now a city with millions of people roaming around. They dig, and so do I. It takes hours to lug a tired body to the surface, but when I do, it is worth it, as long as the hunt is successful.

Last was a drug addict, and before him a woman of the night. Still, there are worse things that can happen.

The tunnel adjoins a large room. Brick and mortar greets me, and one small light gives off a faint glow that just reaches the walls. I smile, pull the fur tighter around my body, adjust the thick lenses, and tap my rings together.

No one will suspect me the way I am dressed today. When they realize what I am, it will be too late, and their body will be dragged down into the crypt to feed me for several days.

The tunnel to the left, that is the one I will use.

A decision in mind, I make my way toward the opening. I stumble. No light shines. The room is suddenly engulfed in darkness. For the love of the almighty! I cannot see in the dark. That is when the power goes out.

Falling from the Sky

The world never saw such a tragedy as befell it yesterday. Harlom's World, desolate with a sparse population, will never be the same.

It was the ship, careening in orbit. Some asshole found the pilot's frequency and broadcast the whole thing for everyone to hear. It was not until the night sky lit up, that we knew what happened.

"Jake!" Nothing wakes you up faster than your wife's panicked voice. "Your caster is going off. They have a problem." Barb is shaking me.

I open sleep-encrusted eyes and push myself up. A cold floor greets me, and a swift swipe of my hand turns off the alarm on my night table. Voices pierce an otherwise quiet night.

"I'll take it in the other room, Grace."

The slight chirp of the AI acknowledges the command. I trip over the cat on the way out of the bedroom. It howls and skitters downstairs.

"I'll kill that fucking thing—"

"You touch Mittens, and that hand will be gone the next day."

She's not joking. Life has not been good to us over the last few weeks. This may be enough to divorce us.

I decide to take the call in the spare room converted into an office.

Grace fills me in as I make my way, "Flight 3445 is coming in hard."

I wince as Grace turns on the lights.

"Visual?"

"Yes."

The ground shakes.

"We are in line with the flight path. They entered orbit three minutes ago. The drive went critical."

I look out the window. Streaks of fire rain from the sky like scattered embers from a cigarette. A fan must have blown.

"Any idea what caused it?"

"Rocks. A number of asteroids were in the flight path."

I swear a guitar is falling in the debris. "Anyone make it to the life pods?"

"Only one pod jettisoned. Initial scans from the internal system show a child clutching crayons and a toy bug made out of wood. She has a simple dress with purple slippers. She is clutching flowers and playing on a tuning wheel."

"Next you'll tell me she has a million in a sack, and a measuring cup with a cookie cutter."

"Don't be silly, Jake. She didn't fall off the Empire State Building." Barb enters and sits beside me, perm rods still in her hair. "Is it bad?" Her voice switches to a caring tone, just like a flashlight brightens the dark. She pushes a seashell from last summer's trip aside and leans against the desk.

"Bad. Seems only the child survived."

The display starts running through the passenger manifest, and Barb cries.

I touch her hand. "Such a loss of life, falling from the sky."

Disposal

The woman had been stunning, with long golden hair glistening on diminutive shoulders. Her angular face and high cheek bones more elfish than normal. I surmise that's why he tried.

I'd been convinced by the honesty of Jacob's testimonial that he would no longer feed on humans. But today's call told me it was a lie. I'm disappointed in him. I'll just charge extra.

Jacob informed me he had a date yesterday night. He'd encountered a woman, and escorted her to dinner. She'd given him all the signals that sex was in the cards, and he was prepared with this motel room. She did not expect what would happen when they were alone. No one could have.

The once quaint room was now in a shambles. A broken lamp, strewn sheets, bloody bathroom floor, and a heavy odour of spoiled meat. The two large bites on the woman's neck could be identified by anyone, so why did he put her in the bathtub with a blow-dryer but not run the water? Did he think it hide the violence of her death?

With a shake of my head, I make my way to the truck. The job is not the most rewarding, but the pay is outstanding. Each client needs a professional to clean up after their dinner – otherwise, they'd be discovered. So my services are always in demand, and I am busy these days. I glance at my watch: just after 3 AM. It's been over 24 hours.

The hydrofluoric acid will liquefy the body as well as the tub. I will need the plastic barrel. Dissolving will have to be off site, and at a premium.

I realize the electric chainsaw will make fast work of the corpse, but today I decide to grab a handsaw to cut the limbs in silence. I place the tool in the barrel, whistling a soft tune as the morning's work begins. First, I drape plastic around the walls of the bathroom to make clean-up that much easier.

Dismemberment is not difficult. Cutting at the joints is the most sensible approach and since the body is already exsanguinated, there is little splatter. I place the parts into the plastic barrel: arms, legs, torso and finally the head. I stare into the vacant eyes. She's packed tighter than a fighter pilot in a cockpit. I secure the lid in place. Little room is left; that means less acid and more profit. It is all about the numbers.

I roll the barrel out of the room and into the back of my van. With the lamp replaced, the clean-up can begin. I work methodically, removing the plastic and washing down the bathroom. I use ammonia to clean the surface and replace the sheets to prepare the room for the next occupant. Finally, I vacuum to suck the last remnants of evidence away.

Satisfied, I lock the room, close the van doors, and buckle up.

The Fire Was Getting Closer

The fire was getting closer to the castle," Jess began. "The king, once a powerful mystical being from the underworld, put forth such an effort of magic to stop the blaze that he sat slumped in his chair, exhausted."

Young Billy yawned. "Keep going, Mom, I want to hear the whole story."

"But you only ate half your dinner, so you only get half a story." Jess rose, brushed her lavender skirt straight.

"I don't like salmon," Bill wined.

"Well, maybe just a little more." Jess sat back down on the edge of Billy's bed, squashing the plush duvet. "The king let out a decry to the magician's guild that the entire world could hear his effort. With one powerful spell, they sent a team of mages to officiate during the destruction of the kingdom."

"Why would they do that?" Billy tilted his head, brow furrowing. "And what does that word mean?"

"Which word?" Jess asked.

"Decry?"

"Oh, that word. I thought it would be a little heavy for you. To decry is to complain. So the king complained to the magician's guild. Just like you decried about having salmon for dinner." Jess smirked.

"Then why not just say complained?"

Jess thought about that for a while. "I guess a writer likes to use fancy words, like decry or officiate." She stood again. "It's past your bedtime, Billy. You'll need to close your eyes and get some sleep."

"Will you finish the story tomorrow?"

"I guess that can happen." Jess walked toward the door. "Just remember to eat all your food next time."

"Even salmon?" Billy's face scrunched up.

Jess blew out the candle. "Even salmon." And with that, she left her young son to sleep the sleep of ages with the glow of an approaching fire outside the castle wall.

The Old Pirate

The sniffle caught my attention. Old Captain Jack, the latest plunder piled in front of him, sits in the tavern, tears watering down the mead he held in an old, dirty hand. The air, thick with the sickly sweet odor of vanilla and allspice, holds the secret of his heart, just like the charcoal sketch between his grimy fingers. I see a story there, though no one will ask him. His other hand wipes away dampness, leaving a clean trail of skin in its wake.

"He killed her, ya' know."

"He loved her, ya' know."

Rumors flew around faster than flies in an outhouse. Nothing confirmed and everything was speculation. Someone has to ask him, but who.

"His ship is with Davey Jones."

"The crew left him on an island."

That could be it. The crew, deciding Captain Jack was no longer needed, left him on an island somewhere with only the woman he loved. No, that couldn't be it. There must be more to the tale than just that.

The old pirate stands, chair grating across the sawdust-covered floor. He picks up one of the dablons and dents it with his eye teeth. A silence moves about the tavern as he does this act. Everyone turns to face him, but nothing escapes his lips except a sigh. He drops his weary body back onto the chair and tosses the coin to the barmaid, making a circular motion with his finger to signal drinks for the room one more time.

"He'll feed us all night if we stay."

"He'll open up about it sooner than later."

Jack finishes his mead then pushes back the chair again, shaky legs taking his weight. The look of despair is plain to see. Eyes half closed, focusing on the floor, he heads to the fireplace. "To women!" His voice booms across the tavern and echoes back to us. With an arm still strong after fifty years, he hurtles the flagon into the flames.

We all wait for the upcoming story, but old Captain Jack will have nothing to do with it. He spins on his heel, walks to his table, and scoops out some coins from his pouch. Not a lot, but enough to make anyone think of cutting his purse for them. He motions the barmaid over, takes her hand and whispers in her ear. She blushes and he kisses her passionately.

As he releases her from his grip he motions toward the remaining treasure. Enough to buy a small town. He then turns his back and strides out the room, leaving us all wondering about the sketch in his hand.

Fluffer

I'm a little cold, lying on the bed totally naked. The way she'd put the plastic sheets over the mattress should have warned me, but you are blind to things like that when sex is promised. That's the reason I let her handcuff me to the headboard like a common criminal.

The cat jumps onto the bed and prances. I want to say something, but the image of the woman standing there with a finger pressed to lips comes to mind. Say nothing. So I try to keep away from the wet, cold nose that quietly explores my hip. A little shimmy of my buttocks takes me away, and the queen struts down the mattress like a fashion model. I can hear the cat purr.

The handcuffs binding my feet are tight. The cat walks over my right leg and sits by my knee. A paw reaches, but all I see is its back. The cat is less than a foot away from something important to me, and there is nothing I can do.

A tail flips about, knocking against my manhood, and I grit my teeth, trying to will an overly excited body not to react.

Ice cubes. Antarctica. Winter snow. Not enough. Alice Cooper. Michael Berryman. Marty Feldman. Rosie O'Donnell. Oh no, my fat girl fetish is triggered. A body starving for sex responds. I pray to God the animal doesn't turn around.

The cat stands, but does not look at the small fleshy scratching post behind it. I close my eyes and mumble a prayer. It's not something I do much, but today the belief that an almighty being will protect me from harm is the only thing keeping me from hysteria.

A harsh tongue slides over my ankle. I clench my jaw tight and imagine teeth shattering from the tension.

The cat jumps down and meows its way out the door.

Then, I hear her voice. "Is he ready, Fluffer?"

Fries Well Done

I remember watching Bill pick up the hammer in his old, gnarled hand. With a quick chuckle, he tossed the tool into the air, then caught it without effort.

"Something you will learn to do"–a glint of patronization fills his voice–"is to always watch the head of the nail."

This was the third time Mom and Dad had hired the carpenter. This year, it was a kitchen remodel. Bill stripped the cabinets out, pulled up the linoleum tile, and yanked out the sub floor. I was only seven, and to watch such a magician at work fascinated me. A practice board laid in front of me with nails jutting out. It was lunch, and Bill said he would take me to The Real McCoys if time allowed. The only thing he made me promise was not to put vinegar on my fries.

"You got that? No vinegar," he said. "It smells up the truck."

He once again made me promise not put the foul liquid on my fries.

"Your mom got her card yet?"

I shrugged. Mom always talked about getting her First Nations' card in order to avoid paying taxes, but struggled to prove her native heritage. "Give it to the man," she would say staring at a stack of paperwork, "and he'll give it right back to you, and more."

"Too bad. I could have made you buy lunch." He placed the hammer in the holder around his waist. That old, beaten up leather belt held everything he needed and then some. I kidded him once about it holding his teeth until he smiled and pulled out a set of dentures. "My emergency pair," he explained with a wink.

"Well, don't worry. A good carpenter uses screws." He dropped one into my hand. "Here, put this one through that board of yours. One trick is to add a dab of carpenter-glue to it; that way the thing will never loosen or squeak."

He watched as my inexpert hands fumble with the task of picking up the screwdriver and the task. Soon, the screw was in, albeit askew. With a smile, he nodded. "Next time, I'll get you to use a drill to drive it home."

My stomach growled.

"Guess you're hungry." He stood, stretching to his full height of over six feet, a giant to a small child. He said God made him tall so he could easily change light bulbs. "Let's get some fries."

We ambled out to his old Chevy. The radio, stuck on some country station, played in the background while he talked. "Remember, get them to really cook the fries well. That way they're almost like potato chips. And gravy, if they have it. No vinegar."

I was a kid in the early '70s, a time when innocence abounded. Children played outside until dark. Bill always had words of wisdom, and since that day, I've always ordered my fries well done and smothered in beef gravy instead of vinegar.

March Break

The morning dew crystallized overnight in the cool air of Kazabazawa. Dad said it would even do so during summer, but this March brought out the true beauty of my Uncles large acreage.

We traveled for over six hours from our Scarborough home. Mom packed jellybeans for the trip along with sandwiches containing that salty, dried Italian meat she so loved. As we crossed into Quebec, the vinyl seat of the car caused my back to sweat, making the t-shirt rub against my skin like sandpaper. Dad always listened to his classical music station, but after Renfrew, all we heard was country music and the whistle of wind passing by our slightly opened windows.

Being only seven at the time, I could not appreciate the sprinkling of rosemary Mom put on her homemade bread, but came to enjoy it later in life.

Six hours is an eternity to a child in 1971, and being cooped up beside my brother did not help my mood. The only true revelation came many years later, looking in retrospect, and longing for a simpler life.

We arrived at Aunt Linda's and Uncle John's old farm home just after 5 PM. They hugged and fawned over us, though I had only met them a few times. Aunt Linda, a large loving woman, busied herself in preparing the evening meal while Uncle John walked us around the small, cleared area. He pointed out the leveled section and explained to Dad, my brother Gary, and me, his plans to build their retirement home fifty feet away from the main building, turning the old farmer home into a garage and workshop.

The small pond, easily covering two acres, stood two-hundred feet away. As I watched the shoreline, a great lumbering bear parted the reeds across from us. John smiled.

"'e be the one I'm getting tomorrow." His thick New Brunswick accent, more French than anything I'd ever heard before, lumbered out. "'e'll fill the freezer for at least six months."

An old, wooden, dilapidated barn became our next stop. Four rabbits hung from nails hammered into a support beam. "Letting 'em shit out," was Uncle John's response to my querying eyes.

To this day, I remember the time spent with Linda and John, always reminding him of his promise to take me to the "butcher shop" far into the woods on his vast estate. He always points to the old 1950 Chev parked out back, saying the beast can still make the journey, but the ancient windows no longer roll up to keep out the cold.

We enjoyed the first meal with them that night. I never really came to appreciate the taste of wild rabbit, but the thought of my enjoyment that week in March between studies still holds a special place in my memories.

Fresh Meat

The stained glass window projected a kaleidoscope of color on the floor as Sonia ran through the church. Her breath escaped. The cascade of color moved as the sun slowly rose in the air. Empty benches could hold the one she was looking for in the abandoned church.

Which way? It was a desperate plea to make a decision. They would be waiting.

With her heart beating frantically, she sprinted to the pulpit, pistol held ready. Water leaked down her shaking hand, but Sonia ignored it. Last week, they had traveled north, taking a hot air balloon across the river to explore a cave. Its dingy darkness let the imagination flow, though not as much as the church with the cobwebs dangling from the ceiling.

He must be here.

Movement caught her gaze, and she looked toward the deteriorating red fabric draped over the altar.

What ceremonies happened here?

A tinkle of glass hitting unyielding floor pulled her thoughts to this instant. A blur obscured the light from the window, and she glanced up, not knowing what would cause such. A sense of foreboding encompassed her, melded greens and blues from the window reeled her mind as a shadow crept past the corner of her eye.

She spun, expecting the worse, but a small bird fluttered to the rafters.

Not here. I'm sure I saw him enter.

Sonia crept forward, stepping over refuse, climbing over the steps for a better view.

A shatter. She turned. Crouched. Raised her weapon and glared toward the window. Nothing.

I'll find him.

The sun cast through the remaining stained glass, glinting toward her. A mocking sight, taking away her ability to see clearly in the receding light.

Was that brown hair?

Wetness exploded on her back.

Exasperated with herself, she lowered her weapon and stomped her feet until she faced her brother. Brandon smiled at her.

"I win!"

"Not fair!" She raised her gun, ready to return the wetness that stained her dress. "We said no to the church, but you came in here anyway."

"It's war. Nothing is fair…" He stopped to glance over her shoulder.

"I'm telling Mom you came in here."

Without a reply, Brandon lifted his pistol, but not at her. Somewhere over her shoulder was the aim point. His small body trembled. Gun held in an unsteady hand.

Sonia turned. With a mind racing in terror, she glimpsed the horror in the window. A long tongue darted across cracked and weathered lips all but obscured by a long ratty beard. Disease and rot floated into the church as a voice old and crackly spoke out the evil thoughts it held. "Fresh meat."

A Sense of Loss

Quin monitored the cryogenic tube. He checked all 1,834,744 tubes. At the start of the journey, 2,000,000 tubes resided under his care, but 165,256 tubes malfunctioned. He agonized over this inconceivable happening.

Bot 230A disengaged from the charging station at Quin's command. It sped down the corridor into the hold containing nine-hundred and seventy-four suspended people, heading for tube 230-CA-0277. The tube, dark with no internal lights, appeared pushed out from the receiving socket by five millimetres.

A puzzle - how did this happen? Quin diverted a bulk of his processing power to the problem.

Quantum
Ultimate
Intelligent
Nano
Technology
Inductive
Network

Quintin, or Quin for short. The final evolution of the computer on Earth. Perplexed by a puzzle. One of his thousand processors checked the ships course. Only 3,433 years, 223 days, 4 hours, 22 minutes, and 17 seconds before deceleration. He mused, as sometimes he did, if a dominant life form could take hold on the planet. The one planet the human race found that could support their life. If that life would evolve into something like theirs, would it also destroy the planet?

The musing, running on processor twelve, ended. Quin routed an algorithm to rewrite code, fix the issue. It was the same code he used to give his "brain" dreams.

Having operated for 567 years, 13 days, 6 hours, 55 minutes, and 34 seconds he performed algorithmic corrections to his code on a continual basis. Programmers of his original instructions would be baffled.

Quin instructed the bot to push the tube into the receiving socket. A beep sounded. Connections engaged. Red lights blinked, turned green, then back to solid red. The person occupying tub 230-CA-0277 had not survived time away from the connection. Another to recycle. Another to dispose of. Another into the biomass to feed the ones who wake.

After 567 years, 47 days, 12 hours, 32 minutes, and 11 seconds, tube 10-BD-0755 disengaged from the retaining struts. Quin monitored as it happened. Bot 10C charged down the corridor into the holding area. It did not stop to examine the readouts or query the main system. Instead, the bot pushed the tube back into place as instructed. The metal clank echoed through the ship. The bot waited.

Red lights blinked. Green lights flickered. Then all the lights went solid red. The life in the tube would not revive.

Quin ordered the bot to pull the tube free, examine the receiver, and report. He pondered about the last thoughts going through the person's mind when the tube released. "Oh, bullocks! Now I'll never get to walk on grass."

No, not everyone wanted to walk on grass. Maybe the man piloted planes and would have moved people from one continent to the next? The man could have been a world class chef willing to make sure all the people on board received a fantastic meal. Curiosity swelled. He needed to investigate the information. A query went to the passenger database. Das, Sumon. Age thirty-three. Neurosurgeon. Bangladesh. Accepted 2455, November 15th. Blood O Positive. Defect in Chromosome 20, gene 758. IQ 143. Married to Das, Chandni. Father of Sumi, Anika, Rimi, Nazir. Parents deceased. Seven relatives listed on board. Further details available.

Quin stopped examining. Time lapsed slowly. This passenger would be missed.

Over the next nine-hundred and forty-five years, 2,583 tubes malfunctioned. Quin sent bots through the ship, not spending processor time with concern over which section they went to. CA bots scurried to PT locations while PR bots dodged into NE. Bots now spent so little time charging and repairing that some ran so low on power and they barely made it back to their charging stations. Lights dimmed unexpectedly. Pressure fluctuated.

After 1,587 years, 3 days, 22 hours, 5 minutes, and 34 seconds, Quin sent bot 10C through the US section and ordered it to stop. The device halted immediately. A small seam appears, and two halves of a circle opened toward the ceiling. One 360 optical camera protruded and bot 10C transmitted. Quin was puzzled.

"Bot 10C, what is that?" Quin sent a command to query the database on Earth's wildlife.

"Unknown," the small bot transmitted back.

"Analyze." Quin realized the small bots had limited capacity due to size. He placed one CPU on standby, then commanded it to restructure the small devices for increased capacity and awareness. "Composition?"

"Biomass."

"More information needed."

"Biomass."

Quin recalled the bot.

After 1587 years, 12 days, 2 hours, 33 minutes, and 6 seconds another tube ejected with a bot recording the same incident. Quin replayed the recording, analyzing every digital frame. A microsecond before the tube popped out, there was a puff of smoke at the socket. He surmised it to be a short.

Quin dispatched a bot.

The small device sped down the corridor and into the cargo area. The explicit instructions pushed into the automaton buzzing wildly. Investigate.

Once at the pod, the bot pulled out it out and illuminated the connection socket. Each part gleamed back as if recently polished. Every connector pin correctly in place. A black scorch mark marred one corner, the same as every one of the pods that ejected. The warning light went off.

Quin instructed the bot to focus on the scorch mark. He watched in earnest as the focus point of the bots recorder zoomed in on the surface. Puzzlement grew in him on what could cause such a mark.

Two small antennas protruded slowly from the hole. The small head came forward next, followed by a dark brown body supported on six legs. With a quick clicking of its tegmina, the cockroach scurried down the receptacle, past the ash remains of a distant relative, and toward the prize - a female of its species.

BONUS

The Hordes

Broken World

Book I

A Hot Day

The traffic stretches from Whitby as far as I can see. A quick glance at the dash shows the time as 30 minutes past when my ass should be sitting at my desk. Shit's going to hit the fan on this one. If the sun would only stop killing us this summer we might be able to survive.

It's July 3rd, and yesterday saw a record temperature – just over 43 °C or a little cooler than hell. Sitting in traffic on the highway puts everyone at egg-frying temp. I play with the air conditioning, hoping it can keep up with the demand. Just one more summer, that's all I need the Focus to last.

Three cars are on the shoulder. Blue, black, and silver. I keep my attention on the road, not looking at the argument or the one passenger grasping at the others through an open window. In this heat, who would keep their window open anyway?

The check engine light flashes on then off. The motor's fan starts to whine and a quick glance at the temp brings out a sigh. Almost all the way into the red. Great. Another shitty day, and now I'll cook even more. I turn off the air, push the heater all the way to "Kill me now," and flip it on. The lava pours out and I roll down a window. This is really going to suck ass. What a great way to start a Monday. How much shittier can 2023 get?

It takes two hours to get just past Pickering. Normally, I would fly through in under twenty minutes. Three more cars sit on the shoulder of the highway with steam coming from under their hoods and, as I pass them, the road opens up. The dashboard clock reads out 9:37 as the green glow fights to escape the glare. So much for being early.

I pull off the highway at Markham Road and battle my way to the college. A few minutes later and the Focus sits in my parking space, engine not stopping even though I've removed the key. For a few seconds it chugs, sputters, refuses to give up life, then it's as quiet as can be. Sweat stains cover me from collar to socks. I'm not worried. No, I have another change of clothes sitting in my office. The idea of cool air conditioning floats through my over-heated mind. This is a great day to take advantage of being the IT manager.

The college employs multiple chillers and redundant power supplies for our computer room – thank God. Nothing beats the heat and humidity more than the good old fashion need to keep the systems running. It takes only a few minutes for me to make my way into the secured room and sit down, undo my shirt another button, and pulled off smelly shoes.

Racks and racks of servers blink green and yellow lights between me and the outside world. This is my safe place. So I pull out the bag containing my "EMERGENCY" clothes, kept stored in the bottom drawer, and change. One of the more interesting things about IT people is we find everything useful. From small throw-away hand towels to big boxes, we find a use for everything. I clean up and look better than if traffic had moved quickly.

Once clean, there's little to do but sit back and wait for something to happen, or the end of the day, whichever comes first. Usually the shifts are uneventful. The odd ping from a server in Turkey or something. Nothing we can't handle.

But the lights go out.

Emergency floodlights switch on. A red glow fills the server room as I pull on my pants. Only one monitor works during brownouts, so I walk over to it and query the system with a few key strokes.

Nothing.

This shouldn't happen. Even if everything is down, there must be a return of how the generators are doing. I type the command again to query the system on the power status. Nothing but a blank screen and blinking curser responds.

Not wanting to show the definition of insanity, I grab my shoes and head to the door. Times like these, the chillers go to half-power. Operating procedure says to monitor the temp outside the room and open the doors if it is cooler outside than in, stationing a fan for air flow. So I go to the door, stare at the thermostat outside and compared it to the one inside the door. I will the one at the door to stay down.

It takes 23 minutes for the first backup power supply to start beeping. Not a nice light beep, but a throaty nagging mother-in-law one. I check it out and decide to turn the alarm off. Nothing I can do in here and the system it controls is redundant.

Something bangs against the door. I spin around and hurry toward it. This time of year usually sees very few people on campus, so how would someone know I'm in here? Curiosity forces me to investigate. The noise becomes furious with the sound of a slapping hand against glass.

When I come out from behind one of the server racks, standing at the door, eyes wide, stands a small Asian girl. Her long hair appears wild from wind and she's sweating, but that could be from the heat. One hand bangs against the thick, reinforced window while the other turns the handle frantically. I read her shirt while walking to the door, trying to make it appears as if I'm not staring at her breasts. "Asian Smart". At least it gets a giggle from me.

I hit the intercom. "Yes?"

Nothing. I can hear muffled yelling but can't make out what she's saying.

Once again I hit the intercom. "You have to press the button." I point to the side of the door.

Her hand slams against the intercom. "Help! Let me in! They're coming!" Her voice holds no accent and the shrill sound grates against my already raw nerves.

"I'm not allowed to. If you want, the nurse is also on emergency power and she can…" Her gaze moves to the right and I follow it. Hell walks toward her. Not really hell, but something that probably crawled out of it just a few minutes ago.

Jesus, one of the grounds keepers I used to smoke with, walks toward the girl, about twenty paces away. Walks is a strong word. Lumbers is better. His black hair hangs loose just like the arms on either side of his body. A long gash down the side of one cheek ends just before his wide open jaw. No blood drops from the wound and his milky eyes only stare straight ahead.

I open the door, pull the girl inside, and slam it shut. She hugs me. Frantic sounds come from her mouth but she speaks so fast I can hardly make anything out. Probably because nothing separates her words as she speaks. I just stare at the door as Jesses bumps up against it.

"Holly fuck!" I hit the intercom. "Are you okay, Jesses?"

As if to answer me, Jesses bumps his head against the glass and tries to walk through the door. If it wasn't for the heat emanating from the girl's body, I might forget about her. No, probably not. The scent of musk along with fresh sweat cloaks her. If I could smell fear, she'd reek of it.

"He's dead," she says, staring at the door. "Oh God, oh God, oh God." She finally lets go of me. "What the fuck have I done!" Her hand rises as she lowers her face. "It's all my fault!"

"What?" Yeah, I've had great aspirations about getting an Asian girl into the server room – a geeky one who'd really appreciate the pure power of all the processors in here. Now, with one basically melting before me, I really turn on my inner Einstein.

She grabs handfuls of her hair. "I killed him."

"I'm sure that's not true." I gesture to the door. "He's there, still walking about."

"You don't understand." She breathes in a shuddering breath. "I pulled into a parking space. Turned up the stereo. My foot came off the break and hit the gas." She points to Jesses. "He flew back from the curb. That gash… I did that." Tears build in her eyes. "I checked him

132

and there was no pulse, no breathing, no heartbeat. I called 911 and cops were on their way. I waited as all his blood spilled out and he died!"

I stare, mouth agape, watching this small girl explain how Jesses, who bangs on the door now, died just outside. A deep breath rattles into my lungs and I shake my head. "You probably just dazed him or something." Taking her hand, I approach the door and hit the intercom. "Jesses, are you okay buddy?"

I can just make out moaning from the other side.

"He's fucking dead!" Her voice approaches shrill as she sinks to the floor.

I catch more movement in the background. A few other people mill about, and another person, with what appears to be bullet holes in his torso, approaches. I recognize him as Dr. Harper, a middle aged man who teaches molecular chemistry. His lab coat is a muddled red instead of the pristine white he loves, only rivaled by the jaundice pallor of his complexion. As he stumbles forward, he drops a severed arm and opens a blood stained mouth. Cloudy eyes stare at me as he bumps into the glass door.

"Shit." I show my waning intelligence once more, but the point comes across.

My guest sobs on the floor. I only wanted to spend the day surfing the net and watching videos, but it seems the whole world has gone to hell.

Without thinking much about it, I help the girl to her feet and lead her deep into the server room. We walk with a quick pace, past racks and air vents blowing somewhat cool air.

The ground shakes and a muffled explosion rumbles through the air.

"What the fuck was that?" she cries out.

I stop, pull her around to face me. "You need to calm down or we'll get stuck in here. Understand?"

She nods.

"Good." I glance about. "What's your name?"

133

"Ming, but everyone calls me Mindy." She sniffs. A tear runs down her cheek.

"Okay, Mindy it is. I'm Steve." I hold out my hand. "Glad to meet you."

She takes my hand and gives a little squeeze. I guess something tells girls to trust me. It's the big brother syndrome and why I'm still single.

I lead her to the emergency exit, but stop. The glass brick wall shows a bunch of shapes lumbering around or just standing there. Something warns me to check first.

With a quick glance, I find a server keyboard and monitor, pull them out, and hit a few commands. Soon, there's a window on the screen showing the security camera feed from the hallway. My eyebrows raise, they're still running, and a smile twinges at the corners of my mouth. In the hallway is a scene from Dante's. Three bodies are on the ground and a number of people rip away at the flesh. After seeing Dr. Harper's snack, there's no way I'm going out there.

"We're trapped," Mindy says.

"You're never truly trapped." I scan the cameras, check for any escape. "The lab."

"The what?"

I tap the monitor. "The lab. Twenty metres that way." With one finger, I point to the south wall. "We can lift the raised floor and get into it."

"And what? Wait?"

"No, not that bad." I take her hand and head to the south wall. "Once we're in there, the emergency door opens to the outside. My car is parked nearby. Do you have a cell phone?"

"Duh, of course." A little ting of are you for real enters her voice. She pulls out one of those huge phones all the teens and under twenties are using. "Network is down."

"No signal? How about data?"

She taps a few times. "Nope, nothing."

134

I pull mine out, not even wondering if it works or not. "Same here." With a swipe I change it to the college network. "Internal's up."

She shakes her head. "Not for me."

"Faculty," I say, as if that explains why, and it does. The look in her eyes says she pieces it together, like most do, that there are two signals in the college: one for students and a secured one for the faculty to use. I connect to the servers, wait for the prompt, and entered my password. A terminal will allow me to up the access, but have to do it before leaving the room. "One sec." I scurry to a terminal, pull up the user profiles, and advance my access to a domain admin. "There."

Mindy stares at me. "What now?"

I lift four floor boards to reveal the main. Cables run toward the south lab. My plan is to follow them and get into the south lab without actually entering the halls.

"I thought these walls were fire breaks," Mindy says.

"Everyone does." I hold out my hand. "After you."

There's only two feet of clearance between the main and raised floor. Each square is about two feet across, or just enough room for a small person to crawl through. I'm not small.

Mindy squeezes past wires and cables in the small space with no issues. I follow her, my back rubbing against the same space every inch. I enjoy the view while the light lasts. But once past a certain point it becomes harder to see, and her firm backside is a blur in the limited light.

Mindy pulls out her cell and uses the flashlight app to see. I motion to follow the cables, indicating where they lead up through the raised floor, and the only other source of light. They would be out of the way of windows and doors. Dust covers a lot of the surface, and once again happiness for no allergies dances in my mind.

As I pass the break area of the main server room, the sound of dragging feet echoes around us. Fists pound against the floor, trying to get through, but soon the noise retreats as we grow closer to our goal. I can imagine the bodies above clambering to get at us. Fingers searching for flesh. No one has ever told me my imagination needs work.

Scraping happens just before I reach the lab break-wall and I swear something on the other side of the floor sniffs. To her credit, Mindy just keeps crawling.

When we attain the main optical lines coming into the lab, I push an access tile aside. Something pushes it back.

Mindy's lips part, but I put a finger against them, feeling the softness. She closes her mouth. I push the tile up and aside again, and as it comes back, I push against it again.

"No fucking way," whispers a deep, harsh voice.

"Frank?" I whisper back. "Frank, it's Steve. I have someone with me. Stop putting the tile back."

The pressure comes off the tile and I push it aside along with a few others. Mindy crawls up first and I follow. Frank just stands there staring at her.

My friend and fellow tech support worker can out stare anyone. His huge bug-eyes stand out in contrast to nothing else about his big body. A broad, flat nose and puffy lips lay on a wide face and even wider neck. Not that he holds a lot of muscle. On the contrary, Frank's body mass make him hard to miss, just like the side of a barn. The college even bought a special chair for him. I'm still shocked I was able to hold the tile back knowing he placed his weight against it.

"Jesus, Steve, you scared the life out of me." He pats his arm with a hand. "Who's the girl?"

"Mindy." She steps back from his leering gaze. "And I'm not a girl."

"Sorry, no offense." Like most of us, Frank pulls back from the starship-like defence Mindy verbally puts up. He cradles an arm and glances about nervously. "Can you give me a hand, Steve?"

"Sure, what's up?" I glance at his arm.

"One of those freaks bit into me before I knew what was going on."

136

He pulls away a hand from the arm and a bandage shows against his dark skin. "Thing broke the skin but little else. Punched the guy and he let go. Stings like a mother!" With exaggerated care, he pulls away the bandage. "Can't get the bitch to stop bleeding."

I guide him to a chair. "Let me get a good look at it."

He sits, causing the chair to squeak out a complaint. The wound doesn't look that bad, but the skin around it already shows puffiness. Swelling is never a good thing. I touch part of it and a green puss dribbles out. Infection? But even though Frank grossly outweighs most people, he never smells of stink. Even his breath, which most people ignore, does not offend. It's one of the reasons why we're friends. That and he's the only one I don't have to watch when he rolls dice during a game of D&D.

"It's not that bad," I say to him.

"Oh, come on. I know what bad looks like and I'm sure green isn't supposed to come out of me from the arm."

Mindy looks around my side. "Didn't you guys take first aid or something? I thought all faculty had to be certified."

Frank Points to it without lifting his head. "Only if you have exposure to the students. Other than that, we can maybe put on a bandage without cutting ourselves. Probably, that is."

Mindy grabs the kit off the wall. "Great. Two geeks and no nurse." She picks up a bandage and a small bottle of peroxide, then helps clean the wound. "Guess I'll just have to rely on what Mom taught me."

Mindy does a good job with the wound. She cleans it up but uses the last of the peroxide on it. Must sting for Frank, who shows great restraint, flinching little. Man it bubbles and fizzes. The green stuff starts weeping again but a couple of gauzes later and Frank can stop holding the arm. She steps back and admires her work.

"Mom would have put an ointment on it or something. Since we don't have anything like that, just cleaning it will have to do." Mindy squeezes his arm. "You'll be okay."

137

"Thanks," Frank says. I swear he's blushing, but sometimes you just can't tell.

"Are you feeling okay?" Mindy stares up at Frank, her hand lingering on his pudgy arm.

"Yeah, just a little chill." Frank crosses his arms with a shiver. "We keep these rooms so cold."

Mindy glances down, takes her hand away from his arm and crosses hers. "Maybe we should get out of here?"

Both turn toward me. Why, I don't know. Frank maybe thinks I'm senior to him, but really, we were hired on the same day. Mindy could be looking toward me for guidance, knowing she's a lot younger than I am. Not by much, probably, but yes, a little.

"We could make it to my place. At least it's out of the city." I scratch my head. "Not sure how well my car will perform, and Mindy's is out front and in a little bit of a wreck." Frank smiles and I know what's going through his head about the girl. "What about your car, Frank?"

"I rode my bike today." He glances down at his arm. "Guess that's not happening this afternoon."

"Well, my car it is." I stare at Frank. "Which way to the emergency exit?"

Muggy and Hot

Mindy and Frank just keep staring at me, as if I'm supposed to know what to do. I'm blank. Not a thought in the world. First apocalypse for me, so how should I know what to do? So, I stand.

"Which way, Frank?"

He snaps out of whatever thing his mind is busy contemplating and points to the wall behind me. "Just down the line of servers there." He drops his arm and looks toward Mindy. "How good are you at heights?"

Mindy tilts her head a little. "Good, why?"

"The stairs are down."

I stop half way to the door. "What?"

"The stairs are down," Frank calls out to me.

I glance back. "Those things are attracted to sound."

"Fuck," Frank says. "No wonder they kept coming at the doors and wall."

I stop and face him. "What? Why?"

"They don't flinch when you bang on stuff." He shrugs. "Most things run from banging."

Mindy tugs at Frank's arm. "What'd you mean the stairs are down?"

"It means they're down. What else?"

"The pull part is down?"

"No, the stairs are down," Frank says.

I reach the door and glance at the sign about the alarm going off if opened. Well, nothing to do but try it. A push against the bar and the door opens. I look down.

The absence of the alarm unnerves me, but only for a second. What causes me to whirl is the empty air my foot hovers over. Frank told the truth, the stairs lay in a wreck of twisted metal on the ground. I count ten bodies struggling in the mess of metal, pieces of brown rebar or rot iron sticking out of them. Their hands grasp at the air, heads twisting about, milky eyes searching. A few heads turn toward the door and my hovering foot. Several lumbering bodies cross the small back parking lot and head to the now open door. Vacant eyes fix on me. Icy fingers dance on my spine.

I search the area, not missing anything – even the backed-up traffic on the highway – then close the door, and sink to the floor.

Frank comes over and holds out a Freezie. Probably from his mini-fridge. "No stairs."

I take the stick of flavoured ice water. Grape. Mindy rolls herself in behind on a chair, the casters rattling on the raised floor. She has cherry. Seeing her suck on it throws my thoughts on a tangent for a few seconds before returning.

There must be something in the air, for Frank turns and stares at Mindy as well. She just sits on the chair, knees together and feet apart, sucking on the Freezie and staring at the ground. That is, until she looks up.

"What?" Mindy smiles with innocence, pushing the last of the cherry ice water up the plastic sleeve. "So, can we get down?"

The fuzz leaves me and I stand once again. "We're three stories up and the whole emergency staircase is in a jumble on the ground. Don't know what caused it, but there's a bunch of bodies mixed in with the metal."

Frank breaks out of his stupor. "I bet a bunch of them were climbing the thing, overloaded it, and down it came." He wacks a hand against a thigh.

"Gross." Mindy uses her feet to scoot the chair toward the door. "I wanna see."

She slides the chair up to the door and waits. I take the hint and push

140

against the handle. The alarm sounds.

"Sorry," Frank says. He runs a few feet to a server rack, reaches up, and taps something. The alarm stops. "I bypassed the alarm in case I was late."

A visual of Frank rushing up the fire escape in order to sneak past our supervisor runs through my mind. I think the tilt sign on my forehead is a little too obvious.

"It's only three stories, Steve. I know you like driving and using the elevator but some of us try to actually exercise."

My throat tightens as I stifle a laugh. Mindy and Frank just stare at me. Once I settle, he flips me the finger, then walks down the row of servers. The crash of glass makes him stop. One glass brick was all it sounded like. A dull thump against the raised floor. But that's all it takes. I shake my head and step beside Frank, take his arm and lead him back to the door.

My voice shakes. "We need something to tie together or we'll never get out of here."

It's like I speak a different language. Frank starts to mumble to himself and Mindy scratches her head. Together we probably have an IQ just north of 400, and the common sense of a dung beetle. At least they have their shit together.

So we split up. Each going to different parts of the server room. Mindy lets out a squeak after a few minutes and runs to Frank. Guess he's the one she saw first. I glance to that area and a number of arms reach through the hole where the brick used to be. Several of the bricks around the opening shift a little as I watch. We need to get out of here. Now.

I find Frank and Mindy looking through the same boxes we each searched through before. They have extension cords and power bars strung together and plugged into each other. It takes a second but I realized what they're doing. Making a ladder with the power bars. The only problem – Frank weighs over 100 kg. Mindy could make it to the ground easily, maybe even me. Frank needs to lose weight if he has any hope in hell of using it.

But they keep working. Plug, wrap, pull, tug, and repeat. The whole thing looks laughable. But the jocks will never see it and neither will anyone else.

The jumbled mess soon stretches the length of the room twice over. I watch as Frank lifts one part and Mindy the other. They carry the makeshift ladder to the door and use more power bars to secure it to a rack. A few tugs later and Frank gives Mindy a high five. I just shake my head. Nerds.

The ladder holds. I go down, hand under hand. Not with grace, but at least I make it down. Fingers and hands reach out toward me, missing my leg by centimetres. I want to swat at them but vacant eyes show no emotion.

Mindy starts her decent, one step at a time. For someone as sure of herself while going under the floor, her movement down the ladder is painstakingly slow. I watch, not out of necessity but reflex when a pretty girl cannot tell you're watching.

She hits the ground and smiles.

"Come on, Frank!" she calls up.

I cringe and whisper, "Mindy, they're attracted by sound."

She slaps a hand over her mouth and words come out muffled. "Oh shit!"

Frank starts his downward climb and both Mindy and I hold our breath. I imagine the plugs coming out and Frank tumbling to the earth into the mix of shifting corpses and waiting mouths. Losing Frank would be a killer, and not something I want.

"Hurry," I whisper over and over again. And then his feet hit the ground.

We all stand on firm earth, smiling at each other. My car sits just a few metres away. I lead them. They follow. A body falls out of the door and lands with a splat where we were, parts of it impaled by twisted metal. A loud clanking sounds as another falls, but it stops moving. One long rebar sticks through its head.

"They're fucking lemmings." I pull keys from my pocket with a shaking hand.

Mindy points into the distance. "More are coming. Better hurry."

No gun. No nothing. Damn fire arm laws. We'd be better off if I had a gun, or at least my hunting bow. Then again, the number of people Frank usually pisses off during the day on his bike makes it better the laws are in place.

"Come on man," Frank mutters. "Get that door open and let's get out of here."

It's not like I don't want the door to open. The damn key is the problem. Usually use the remote. "Idiot!" I swear and press the open door button on the little transmitter. The only thing that works perfect on the damn car is the remote.

Mindy slips in the front and Frank pushes his bulk into the back. I press the clutch, jam the keys into the ignition, turn, and pray. A sputter.

"Come on," I whisper. The day is still hot and the windows all closed. We cook in the heat. Frank's deodorant must have given out on the climb, the smell of humanity reeks in the car. One more turn.

The car starts, stutters, almost stalls, revs up, smooths out. I let out a sigh.

"Get this shit-box rolling, Steve," Mindy says, her head toward the window.

Just a few steps away comes one of the student chefs, cleaver in one hand, bloody stump on the other side. His lumbering gait tells me what he is. The cleaver raises into the air.

"GO!" Frank screams.

The cleaver comes down. It hits the car just before the front window. I slam the gear into reverse and pop the clutch. The Focus screams, wheels spin, and we back up. Slow at first, then the tires grab. I shove it into first and take off down the parking lot, dodging the animated corpses as we go.

Mindy points out the front. At first I think it's just at the cleaver still embedded in the hood, but that's not right. As we approach the problem becomes clear. The gate bars our way out of the parking lot. And even though it is only wood, I drive a rusted-out Ford Focus. I remember the ground spikes they installed last year.

"Shit!" Yes, another intellectual masterpiece of a word.

I catch movement inside the guard house. A quick look behind shows a wall of animated death lumbering toward us. They didn't move fast, but it's a large wall of bodies able to just walk in a straight line, not dodging parked cars or following the road.

With not much time to decide on what to do, I step on the gas and pray.

The gate starts to lift, meaning the spikes must be down. Thank God! A womp and screech tell me the wooden arm scrapes against the roof on its way up. A head spins slowly in the guard house and some temp worker seems to wave. I swear to God he does.

We rise into the air and land back down on the road. Damn traffic calming hump at the end of the drive. My back bumper spins away in my rear-view mirror until it comes to rest by the curb. We skid a little before I get the car under control.

I think of all the routes to get home and decide the back roads would be better. Many cars jam the street, but at least they move. The sight of the highway, when we escaped Frank's room, told me to stay clear of them. I do.

Generally it takes me only 40 minutes to get home. Today, because of the traffic and lumbering bodies, I don't get there until the gas gauge light comes on. Seven litres left. Enough to get us one hundred kilometres if we only feather the thing in fifth gear.

My power still works. A quick hit of the remote and the garage door pulls up and out of the way. I back in. A quick swing of the wheel and roll forward. A yank on the parking brake locks the wheels. I pull out the key. The car sputters, knocks, and finally stops.

I put my head on the steering wheel.

Mindy stares straight forward.

Frank barfs.

My nose revolts. "Jesus! What the hell did you eat?"

As if to answer my question, he barfs again. Mindy and I open our doors and scramble out.

"I guess that means you'll be looking for a new car." She pulls at the bottom of her shirt, causing it to stretch over her small breasts.

Of course I look. Still alive doesn't mean not being a perv. She keeps the shirt stretched for a while and it dawns on me what she's doing. I look up and she's smiling.

"Sorry." I glance away after a good eyeful and knock on the rear passenger window. "You okay, Frank?"

If a black man could turn white, that is what Frank looks like. Eyes barely open, lips pale, and a small sheen of sweat on an otherwise shinny brow. "I'll be okay."

To show it, he barfs again. Thank God for the empty grocery bags in the back. It must be just about killing Frank in there. Maybe I can air the car out tonight or something. Right now, it's my only means of transportation in and out of the small town I live in.

I motion Mindy to the door with a hand. "I'll show you around."

She hesitates. "What about Frank?"

"He's been here before."

She nods and follows me into the house.

Air conditioning is wonderful. The blast of cold, about 22 °C, energizes me and puts a spring in my step. Samantha greets us at the door. Her feline howls for attention are nothing compared to the rasp of the tongue she uses on just about everything. The exaggerated black M on her forehead stands out against light brown fur.

The reaction Mindy has with the air becomes more entertaining than the pulling of her shirt. Another stare moment, but I look away before she sees me. At least I hope so. I feel heat on my cheeks.

Mindy bends down and picks up my little ball of fur. "Oh, she's so beautiful!"

"Samantha. Named after a witch." I smile. Chicks dig cats. They dig guys who like cats. Samantha got me laid a few years back before she porked out. Now, at just over 7 kg, her biggest accomplishment is jumping up on the bed at night.

"Can she wiggle her nose?"

For someone I think is just over twenty, Mindy is starting to impress me. "There's no way you can know that show."

She smiles. "My parents loved reruns. Helped teach them English."

I continue with the tour of my home, showing her everything from the kitchen to the upper floor TV room. For obvious reasons I steer clear of the bedrooms. Samantha trudges along behind us. We end up in the basement as the last stop. A mashing of wires run through the support joists with three massive Power Wall stations. I explain about going off the grid after the last big Liberal energy increase, cutting wood in the winter for the fireplace in order to help the geothermal furnace; powering everything from solar. Big investment, but worth every dime. I can run my air whenever I want without worrying about the cost. Even the winters are warm with the fireplace helping out. She nods, smiles, drools. It's a geek thing.

Mindy pulls out her cell and then looks at me. "What's the password?"

She wants the wi-fi password, something I rarely give out. Usually I have time to setup a guest access point to limit download speed and what they can see from my home servers. Today I didn't expect to bring

146

anyone home with me.

Mindy sees my hesitation. "Sorry, just… well, my VOIP doesn't take up much bandwidth and I'd really love to check my mail with the network down."

It's against my better nature to disclose passwords. Working in IT, my guts twist when someone says they're going to write their password down. Come on, write it down? How about just giving someone the pin to your bank card? But then again, I've heard of people putting those on the signature strip.

I've never seen a cute girl beg. That's what she just about does. Hell, she seems about ready to let a tear run down a cheek. I give in. Tell her the password. I can always change it tomorrow. How many of these "corpses" can use their cell's anyway?

"Okay, but it's not connecting." Mindy holds out her phone for me to see.

"Oh, the 'bash' is not the word. I'm an old linux guy, it's the exclamation mark." Common mistake, that's why I always say it the way I do.

"It's connecting. Got signal. That's pretty strong. What are you using to keep the signal strength so high?" Her fingers dash over the cell's small screen.

"The power lines in the home do all the transmissions." I indicate the walls. "The whole house is a transmitter."

She nods. I think I just went up a few notches in her book.

"You think Frank's okay?"

I fall a few of those notches. "Should be." I scratch my head a little. "Let's get him cleaned up. It's the least we can do."

"Probably needs a change of clothes." Mindy follows me up the stairs.

"I don't think there's anything here for him to wear. I could have a look. Maybe he left something last time he had to sleep over."

"Why would he need to sleep here?"

"D & D party. Adults don't drink fruit juice."

She seems to get that, letting out a little giggle.

We make our way into the garage. Frank seems to be still barfing his guts out but that doesn't stop the little fire cracker from opening the door. The poor guy looks half dead.

Frank glances up at Mindy, tries to smile, fails, lulls his head and groans.

I saw Samantha corner a chipmunk one day. The little thing shivered and sputtered, trying to get away from the claws. When a gash was too much, and the blood almost out of its body, the thing seemed to give up on life and look at my cat with resignation to its fate. It was better than the look Frank holds in his eyes. At least the chick monk knew what was happening to it. I don't think Frank has a clue. None of us do. Mindy reaches into the car first. Not sure what she's thinking, all 40 kg of her. Frank tips the scale. It would take four Mindy's to even out the teeter totter, and even then I don't think it would level out. But she grabs his arm and gives a tug.

Frank helps. He raises a hand and pulls against the car door frame, his body straightening up just a little bit at a time. Then, he stands. Or should I say wavers.

I rush over before the guy topples to his knees.

"We need to get him inside." I can hardly believe the heat coming off Frank's body. "Crap, I think we need to get him to a hospital."

"No hospitals," Frank utters, his voice just barely above a whisper. "Just get me someplace to lie down."

"I don't know, Frank," Mindy says. She rushes ahead and opens the door. "If Steve thinks a hospital would be better then maybe we should get you to one."

"Don't think they'd be safe." His breathing settles down, as if he draws more strength by being pushed into movement. "The whole country's going to rat shit so the hospitals will be overrun with people."

Can't argue with his logic. The world does seem to be going to hell and we're just here for the ride. Maybe a lay down is all he needs. Mindy

148

glances over and I look up, shaking my head.

Once inside the house and surrounded by cool air, he visibly relaxes. The bandage on his arm seems soaked with blood so I steer him toward the kitchen table. After a quick explanation of where to look, Mindy goes to the bathroom for bandages. She comes back and removes the blood soaked ones first.

I've seen a lot of crap. Heck, anyone with the internet has seen stuff from rough porn to tortured animals. I've never seen anything like the sight I see as the bandage comes off. Well, it doesn't really come off. Mindy pulls it off. Gently at first, then with a little more effort. Frank doesn't even wince. The skin looks ill, but nothing prepares me for the smell.

Chicken in the Sun

Mindy covers her mouth. I take the bandage away from her and walk into the garage, holding back my stomach with every step. The bio-waste bucket sits on the ground just beside my old beat up truck that hasn't started since last year. I haven't tried to start the vehicle this year, didn't want the disappointment of the thing not running again. The bio container has a good seal, and we won't smell the rotten chicken again.

I toss the bandage and go back into the house to find Mindy trying to clean the wound. She has a roll of paper towel in one hand and a few gauze squares in the other. The latter she presses close to Frank's wound and pushes a little. A sickly yellow-green puss seeps out of the bite mark and she scoops it up. The smell intensifies when she does the action. Chicken left in the sun is all I can think of. That's not saying Frank smells like roses, no matter what his personal hygiene is like. We all spent too much time in my stinky little car.

"You have enough light?" I indicate the curtains drawn tight against the heat.

"Enough," Mindy says. She keeps pushing against the wound and more puss seeps out.

"Do you want any water?"

"Cold. Put ice in it if you can."

I really hate feeling useless. Sitting in front of a computer gives you the feeling of God, knowing at any time you could just press a button and send someone's personal information to anyone. Heck, there were a lot of things I could do at work. World of Warcraft beware! Frank and I control a number of groups. Crap, I had forgotten about the raid we setup for today. I glanced at the time. An hour past the meeting.

Ice clinks in the glass and water spurts out the fridge spout. I move on autopilot while thinking about the day. The glass almost reaches my lips before I remember it's for Mindy.

"Here." I hold out the glass.

"How's your arm feel, Frank?" Mindy presses the bandage against the bite waiting for Frank to respond.

"Better. Less pain." Frank takes a deep breath, flexes the fingers of his bit arm. "My fingers are a little numb."

"Could be nerve damage." I swear at myself for that one. Mindy glares at me from under her brow, an interesting trick for an Asian woman.

"Probably just the swelling," she says. "We should get some water into you."

"Rather have a pop." Frank wipes his brow. "Never really liked drinking water."

Mindy scowls. "Well, you'll drink it today."

I take the hint and get another glass.

"Thanks," Frank says, taking the water from me. "I'll try not to spill any."

Samantha jumps up on an empty kitchen chair, sits down, and stares at Frank. Her ears fold back and those lovely green eyes all but close. She lets out a hiss.

"Sam!" I glare at my cat. She jumps down and runs out of the kitchen, then thumps up the stairs.

Frank shook his head. "What's wrong with Samantha?"

"Who knows?" I walk back to the fridge and pour another drink, this time for me.

The way Samantha acted concerns me. Last time Frank came up to the house she fawned all over him. She even jumped up on his lap while we watched the game, something she never does with anyone. Something's wrong, and I'm punked if I know what it is.

Mindy says something but I don't catch it.

151

"Sorry?"

"I said do you have any more bandages?"

The thought whips through my mind. Probably, but where? "What type?"

"Big ones." Mindy wipes more ooze off Frank's arm. "Think I got it cleaned out real good. Maybe some alcohol or something."

"Peroxide?" I'm sure some of that sits in a cupboard somewhere in the house.

"That'd do." Mindy presses another paper towel against Frank's arm and reaches for her glass. "And some more water."

It only takes a few minutes to find the peroxide, use it for cleaning printer heads. The bandages are another issue. I look all over to find something more than a simple kid's bandage, but nothing stands out. Not the stores in the kitchen or the bathrooms. Downstairs is a bust as well. Not one blood-stopping thing.

They're in the upstairs linen closet, up against the side the door folds into. Almost missed them if it wasn't for the big red cross on the package.

"Found some for you."

I wait a second, then decide just saying something was all I need to do. So down the stairs I go, seeing a four-legged ball of fur run into the closet I had opened. Fine, if she wants to be alone, let her.

Down the stairs and into the kitchen, I glance at the pile of grey-green paper towels on the table. Great, going to have to clean the table as well, not like the cat hasn't been sitting on it all morning, it gets the sun.

"Three sizes in this one." I put the box on the table and grab her glass. "Water or something stronger?"

I watch the internal struggle she goes through. Seems all kids love booze no matter who they are. "Got a beer?"

"I'll take a beer," Frank says.

"No!" Mindy and I say it at the same time. Frank winces.

To the fridge I go and pull out two beers from a micro-brewery I like.

152

Something about the lime taste that gets me. Almost like an English pub beer. I crack the can and hand one over to Mindy. She takes it and smiles. The strange picture on the side makes her brow furrow but she doesn't say anything.

Frank drinks from his glass.

The bandage goes on fast. Mindy wraps it around his arm and ties it off with ease. The discolouring takes a little time to come through so I decide plastic sheets for Frank tonight.

Mindy checks her phone and frowns. "No signal."

I look over. "You on one of those small carriers in Toronto?"

"No, Bell." She swipes at her phone.

"Should be good. Did you connect to my network?"

She swipes the phone again. "Yeah, but the VOIP isn't working."

I dig out my phone, no connection except for the network. A few taps and I realize the outside is cut off. "No internet."

Frank has his phone out, an old dinosaur of a device. He flips it open and shows he has bars. "Old tech keeps working."

Mindy glances at him. "Can I use it to make a call?"

"Sure," Frank says, handing it to her. "Dial 9 to get an outside line." He laughs, then wheezes. "I gotta lay down, Steve. Where you want me?"

"Fold out in the front room." I point. "Let me get sheets on it first."

"I'll help," Mindy volunteers.

"Thanks."

We dig out the plastic sheets and setup the bed. Mindy puzzles over the choice but I mention Frank's wound discolouring the bandage and she nods. After a few minutes the bed holds the big guy and he's snoring softly. I motion for Mindy to follow me upstairs and into the TV room over the garage.

"Nice," Mindy says, looking at the TV again.

"Thanks." I pull out the modem and stare at the lights. The ones leading to the outside world all flash red, the others, green. No internet.

"High def?" Mindy stands before a couch now, eyeing the strange remote on the table.

"4K. Pick it up." I motion to the remote. "It's old, but easy to use."

With the power wall charged and the solar panels collecting, I wasn't too worried about the pull, even with the stereo. Mindy flips everything on and the room comes to life. I cover my ears from the blast of static coming through the speakers. Mindy winces as well.

"What is that?" Mindy tries to cover her ears and looks at the remote. She fails.

"You're on the sat, stopped on a wild feed I picked up last night." I stand and go over, expecting blood to be dripping from her ears. Nothing. "We have to change to over the air." I hit the remote. Sound dissipates. "Better. Flip through and see what's on. Try the news."

Mindy scans the stored channels, frowning at the lack of signal. All the major channels show us is black screen until we switch to the ancient ones. They show old fashion snow. The sound of hissing. Then she hits something. The picture still looks like we stare through a blizzard, but at least we can see it.

A man stands before us on the TV, his words mesh out every few seconds with the static. He proclaims, trumpets, and prostrates himself as the camera follows him along. An evangelist preacher. For some reason, all the channels, except this one, are off. I recognize this guy. His persona is always on the news about how he rips off seniors and seduces the interns. Not a nice character.

We both stare at the screen, hypnotized by the dancing static, hearing only half of what he says. Apocalypse. Hellfire. The dead. Evil. The dialogue goes on as he either thumps a fist into his hand or on the bible. I shake my weary head.

A quick motion to the control breaks Mindy out of the hypnotic preacher. "Nothing else on?"

Mindy scans the channels again and the only one we pick up is the reverend. I hold out a hand and Mindy puts the remote in it. A few minutes later, the TV has scanned the airwaves finding only that channel.

"I'll switch to the sat." The system flips to the small dish on the roof and I scan. Hundreds of scrambled channels show up.

"A lot to choose from," Mindy says.

I change the view and only twelve channels show. "These are the unscrambled ones on Nimiq 1."

Lots to see there. Some fireplace channel, the Canadian Parliament channel, a few other free for now channels and the news.

Crap! The news? I almost missed it.

The station came in off the satellite in dazzling clarity. I turn up the volume once the feed clears. The low tone buzz makes my back teeth vibrate as the words "This is the Emergency Broadcast Signal. Please stand by," flashes on the screen. We wait. And wait.

"I don't think anything is going to happen," Mindy says.

The back of her hand brushes against mine. Amazing what life and death can do to people in such a short time. I glance at her, but she keeps those beautiful eyes staring at the screen.

"I'm sure something will–"

The screen goes black for a second. A rustling of papers comes through the speakers and soon the picture splashes on in full HD quality. I gape at the background images of bodies sprawled on the ground, people shooting into crowds, and the general loss of humanity.

It must've been a live transmission; no one goes in front of a camera to read the news looking as disheveled as this man, but there he sits. The slight shadow across his chin tells us of how long the day has been. I can see the light trace of circles under eyes, far too young to have such. Hands shake as they pick up a few pieces of paper, then put them down. As a thought, he reaches for the glass of water, but the tremors continue to cause his hands to spill it on the papers he had just put down. He clears a dry throat and begins to speak.

"I'm Peter Michaels of the National News Service, sitting in for Philip

Jahad. Today, we are a nation under siege." His breath slows as the few years of training he had kicks in and takes over. "The world is under siege. The Centre for Disease Control in the United States has announced an outbreak affecting North America and Mexico. We're still waiting confirmation from the Public Health Agency of Canada.

"The CDC is warning people to be wary of those stricken by this disease. They may be your loved ones, but being infected takes their mental competence away from them. They may attack you. Be careful of their bite or bodily fluids. If infected, please advise your family and law enforcement. Please do not attempt to enter a hospital, they are currently on lock down in order to protect those who are the weakest among us."

Mindy recovers first. "Jesus!" She squeezes my hand hard. "I really need to talk to my mom." Frank's phone is in her hand again and a small thumb dances across the numbers. It goes to her ear, then down again. She hits the numbers one more time and repeats.

I watch her brow furrow and the corners of her mouth sink. It takes a while for me to see the tear.

"Hold on, what's wrong?" I put a hand on her shoulder.

"Lines are down." She sniffles.

"That's nothing new." I'm really good at helping people feel better. "If the main cell lines are down then the hard lines are probably as well."

Her eyes lift a little and the sparkle is almost back. "You think so?"

I can feel the paint drying around me as I sit in the corner with a dripping brush. "Suuuuurrrre." Samantha rubs against my leg. I bend down and pick her up, offering the little bundle of fur to her. "Cat?"

The giggle tells me I hit the right nerve. She takes Sam out of my hands and hugs the little motor boat. "I never had a pet when I was a kid."

"Hell, you can have her. Keeps me from cleaning the litter box."

The announcer clears his throat and I look over. He's a little less worse for wear but still not that presentable. The set behind him shows several people moving about and a nearby security guard.

"Things are happening that you need to know." He glances to the left. "I know how this will sound, but it has to go out there. The dead are coming back to life."

Another person comes on screen, but his back is turned to the camera. "Pete, you need to stop. They'll pull us."

"Jesus!" I stare at the screen.

"Must be bad if the government is censoring it," Mindy says.

"Jeff, it doesn't matter anymore. The people need to know what is going on." He turns back to the camera. "People, listen to me. The dea–" The signal freezes, blotches. I swear. "–don't try to a he–" Again, we lose signal.

Mindy glances at me. "What is he trying to say?"

"–when you come across someone bitten, ju–"

I flip the channel up and down. The station is still there, but something is trying to block it. "Seems like their signal is being interrupted by something." A few steps to the right and I look out the window. Clouds are rolling in from the west. Dark, nasty weather clouds. "Looks like a storm's coming in."

"–nd try to keep safe. Lock yourselves in a secure home. Don't let anyone in who shows sig–" Pixelisation covers the screen. "–the brain– it stops the–base of the ne–though the ey–don't bu–spinal co–just bod– head trama–" The picture finally gives out to a black screen.

The summer storm rolls in. Wind picks up and light fades. "This is going to be a good one." I turn off the TV. "Best to wait it out. I have movies and such we can watch."

Mindy stares at the TV. "Maybe we should look in on Frank. Make sure he's okay."

"Good idea." I start to head for the stairs. "You coming?"

"In a sec."

"You okay?" There's a welling of moisture in her eyes. Crap, I hate it when chicks cry. "If you want to lay down…"

She wipes at her eyes, gives a little smile, and fights back the invisible demons. "I'll be all right. Just thinking."

I nod. She walks toward me. Down the stairs we go and into the living room.

Fred is sprawled on the fold out. He's still sleeping, even with the sound of the rain. Summer storms can get pretty brutal here. The small town I live in is kind of in a cauldron of sorts. Way back in the early 1800's it used to flood, that is before they put in drainage ditches and paved roads. Now I just get a little water in the basement when a storm is out of the east.

Mindy walks up beside the bed and puts a hand on Frank's forehead. Gingerly, she then pulls back the green stained bandage on his arm. She shakes her head and glances at me.

"I cleaned that well, but it seems to be just as swollen as before."

I come up beside her and look down. The chicken-left-in-the-sun smell slams into me so hard I almost gasp. "His arm looks bad."

Mindy touches around the wound. "Yeah. We should really get him some medical help." She puts the bandage back in place. "I'm not a doctor, but I know an infection when I see one."

Images of my friend losing his arm floats unbidden to my consciousness. Frank would not like that if it happened. Heck, I wouldn't like him to go through that, but what can you do if they decide it needs to be removed in order to save your life?

"Is there anything we can do?" Ask questions. Hunt for an answer. Just like programming. Follow a plan to fix the issue.

She takes a deep breath. "Nothing that I can do. Basic first aid. Mom and Dad wanted me to be a doctor, but dealing with sick people gives me the creeps."

Something I can relate to. I look out the window. "Don't think we're going anywhere soon." Lightning lights up the sky. A few seconds later, thunder rolls across the landscape. I look at Frank. His snore answers me. "Looks like he's at least getting some sleep. You hungry?"

158

"Rather have another beer."

"That can be arranged."

Bump in the Night

We sit and talk in the TV room. Mindy says a lot about her family and how they wanted her to be a doctor. At the fifth beer, my cheeks are tingling and the world starts to make sense. Funny how everything is better with a few beers in you.

The storm keeps pouring down. When the room becomes really dark, I turn on a light and look outside, announcing it to be night time and head to bed. I tell Mindy about the spare bedroom and where to find extra sheets. At least I think I tell her that.

The rain stops sometime during the night and a strange thumping sound wakes me up. It's just my head from all the beers. I stumble to a standing position, still groggy, but nothing a good brushing of the teeth won't fix.

Mindy is curled up with me. Her olive shin glints in the pre-dawn light and I wonder how far we went. It's hard to tell, I like commando. It appears she does as well.

I try to extract myself from our intertwined bodies, feeling myself stir as hands touch the soft skin of her breasts. The biggest problem is my right arm, and Mindy's head resting on it.

A pillow in one hand and the other balancing Mindy's head, I pull away slow, making sure not to jostle her in any way. Long, silky hair follows but the pillow slides under her head and I let out a silent cheer of achievement before slipping my feet out and onto the floor.

Curiosity gets the best of me and I lift the sheet just a little to look at her naked back, then down to her butt. I give myself a mental high five and let the blanket fall back down against her body.

My comfy pants are by the bed so I slip them on, and push reluctant feet into slippers. The clock beside the bed reads 4:45 a.m., just a few minutes before sunrise. Time to put on some coffee.

Mindy's voice breaks the silence and I stop. "Black, three sugars."

"You're supposed to be asleep."

She giggles a little, not rising, but I see the outline of an arm coming up to her head. "What? And miss the show?"

I blush, it's one thing to look, but getting caught is another. "Three sugars?"

"Yes. And something for my head, it's pounding."

There's a thudding noise downstairs, as if someone hit the dining room table. Samantha runs into the room and jumps up on the bed, ears flat, a low growl comes out as she looks toward the door. Her hair is puffed out.

Mindy sits up, sheet falling from her body. "What's wrong with Samantha?"

I look to her, look at the cat, look at her. The light is growing and I can see her even better now. I try looking into Mindy's eyes, but my gaze falls a little south. She giggles. Another thump. Her smile disappears. Samantha growls again.

"Must be Frank. Probably thinks he's an elf and can see in the dark. I'll make some coffee." Hesitation as she looks at my lower body. I glance down to see my soldier standing at attention. Again, heat rises to my cheeks. "Better get out of here to settle him down."

She giggles again, grabs Samantha, and dives back under the covers.

I turn and head to the stairs, making my footfalls loud so Frank knows I'm coming. With a force of will, I think about my boss naked and my arousal dies, quick, but my stomach almost hurls at the image. Going to have to remember that trick in the future.

"Frank?" There's only silence, then a groan. "I'm coming down to make some coffee, want any?"

Two steps down.

DOUGLAS OWEN

"You okay, Frank?"

Four steps down.

"Frank, answer me, will you?"

Six steps and I peer at the fold out. Sheets are crumpled into a mass around a dark form. He's still laying there, but his leg is draped over the edge of the bed to the floor. It thuds against the floor making the sound we heard upstairs.

I'm a coward. Scared of the dark. Dash upstairs when I turn off the lights so the boogie man doesn't get me. Stuff like that. I rush toward my friend and stop a few paces away. The sheets are smeared with the green gunk that came from his arm yesterday. I pull back a sheet and see the puss also covers his body. An arm, once recognizable, is bloated, puffy, and a bluish tint runs its length. Instead of part of his arm looking ghastly, the whole thing gives off a harrowing growl of anger to my senses.

"Frank."

His breath is ragged and gurgles as if he is drinking from a straw with only drops at the bottom of the glass.

Frank shakes, starts to convulse. I reach out with fumbling hands and attempt to stop him from hurting himself. Crap, he's burning up. The heat coming off him is tremendous. The sun would have a hard time warming him this high. The gurgling in his chest grows. He shits himself. The smell is sickening and hits me like a train. I swallow back bile. And as fast as the convulsions start, they stop. His breath rattles out. There is no more struggling or movement. Nothing.

"Frank!"

I shake his shoulders. His head lops to the side. Spittle mixed with blood foams in his mouth and I know we've lost him. I sit on the edge of the bed and hang my heavy head. We were friends. Maybe not the best of friends, but still friends. World of Warcraft and Pokemon and just about any kind of game you could imagine. He even tried to teach me dominoes once.

162

Mindy comes down the stairs and stops. "I heard yelling…" She's carrying Samantha who struggles to get free. One of my old flannel shirts covers her from shoulders to knees, but the front is only buttoned a little. She sits on the stairs and Samantha jumps free of her grasp. I could only imagine the tableau we form.

It lasts a while. Me sitting on the edge of the bed, Mindy on the stairs, Samantha hiding somewhere, Frank decomposing slowly beside me. I remember some of the pranks he used to pull at work. Little things like changing a small line in someone's email signature or making a rom drive open on them. Little things like that to make a person smile.

The brief reflection ends and I stand. A quick tug and the blanket covers Frank's body. I bend my head and mutter a silent prayer for my friend before going to the kitchen. The cat food is in a jar and I scoop out some for Samantha, wondering where she is. This is her happy time. Food time. But my cat seems to have abandoned us. I still fill her bowl and put it down.

Small arms encircle my waist and the press of a body bears on me. I'm not sure what to do, but something has to happen. I reach down and touch one hand. Her body shakes against mine and sniffling sounds fill the room. Maybe something else is wrong but for now all I can think of is getting coffee ready.

"I don't think I could eat." She rubs her head against my back.

A realization comes over me. This woman is bonding to me. I've had girlfriends before, but nothing like this one. She is pretty, smart, sexy, hot. I think we had sex and I never really bought her dinner or took her to a show. How the hell did that happen? The world is a strange place.

I reach for the coffee urn and grinds. Spill in two scoops. Put it down. Pick up the kettle and fill it with water. Plug it in. Wait.

Her arms tighten around me.

"We have to eat." Thoughts of what to make go through my mind. "Then take him outside."

The squeezing stops.

DOUGLAS OWEN

I take a deep breath. "It's not something I want to do either, but we can't leave him in here much longer. The heat…"

Her voice almost breaks. "When?"

"Soon. After breakfast."

"Okay, but nothing big." She squeezes me again.

I push away from the table. Mindy has an appetite and already packed away six pancakes and half a pack of bacon. She eats like someone starving, shovelling forkful after forkful into her mouth. Her coffee is black with three sugars. Sweet, but not overpowering, just like her. How the hell does she stay so skinny?

We talked during breakfast. She's a second generation or CBC as she calls it, Canadian born Chinese. Parents live in Toronto, downtown, where they run a sushi restaurant. She works there in the summer and goes to school the other times. Like she said, they wanted her to be a doctor but it was not in her future. She loves drama and the arts. The biggest claim to fame, she admitted, a commercial spot that aired last winter.

"Got milk?" She laughs and just keeps scooping more food into her mouth.

I stand, motion to the dwindling supply of pancakes. "Do you want more?"

Her fork dashes out faster than the eye can see and the last two are on her plate. A quick movement and maple syrup is poured over them.

"This is enough." She forks another pancake into her mouth, chews, and swallows. "What?"

"I've just never seen anyone eat so much." I take the empty plate from the centre of the table. "Frank says–"

She stops eating. I can't believe I just said that. Frank is still on the pull out, covered by the blanket. Mindy's lower lip starts to tremble.

"I'm sorry." The plate shakes as my hand quivers. "It's just hard to

164

believe he's gone."

Mindy nods, then looks down at the last two pancakes cowering on her plate. "Some cultures bury food with the recently deceased so they have something to eat."

I nod this time. "Sounds like a plan." My scheme for the backyard was almost complete. Just a few more places left to smooth out. But why in the first part of the back? Heck, my property is almost an acre so we could bury Frank just about anywhere. I have plastic to wrap around his body. Keep the animals from eating any part of him.

Images of my friend being dug up by coyotes run through my mind. Their teeth ripping and tearing at his flesh. It makes me sick to think his grave could be desecrated so easily just because I live in a rural area. No, we'll bury him, wrapped in plastic.

"Have you tried your phone yet?" I pull my own out and check for signal. Nothing.

"This morning. No signal." She sits back, lets out a deep breath. "I wish I knew what was going on with my parents."

"I'm sure something will be up later today." I go to the sink, put the dishes in it, and stare at Samantha's bowl. "Things are just a little weird right now."

"No shit." Mindy gets up and puts her plate on the counter.

I reach down, open a cupboard, and pull out a sandwich bag. The pancakes go into it.

It takes us the better part of an hour to haul Frank's body out of the house. Most of that is my fault.

We tried carrying him by arms and legs, just like the old-style grave diggers did. But a dead body is limp, offering no resistance. He slips from our arms and hits the floor. We try again and the same result. No one told me a limp body is hard to carry.

I put the sheet on the floor and together we roll him onto it. Then we

165

drag him through the kitchen and out into the yard. Ten minutes of pulling and we have him exactly where I measured out. I remember something he said to me last year about two feet in either direction and five feet from another, so I pick one of the birch trees and paced out five steps before digging.

They used a backhoe in order to level out part of my back yard. Rocks litter the ground not too far down, so they're a pain. I keep hitting them with each shovel full of dirt. At least I can somewhat muscle them out. Mindy is helping with another shovel and stops just about all the time to see if she got a rock. Thankfully, they are usually small enough to pry out of the ground.

Mindy straightens up, pushes hair from her eyes and looks around. "There's no road noise."

"Sorry?"

"Cars. I don't hear any cars."

I stop digging. Nothing. No dump trucks heading to the pits just north of me. Wind, yes; but vehicles, no. Even in this rural neighbourhood there should be cars running back and forth, I'm just a stone's throw from one of the highways, small though it is.

"Yes, silence." I relish in the moment, then realization slaps my across the face and brings me back to reality. "Silence. Not even a plane or car." Very disturbing. I rub the back of my neck, let the shovel drop, step out of the hole we started. "People should be moving about."

"Come to think of it, I didn't even see any lights on anywhere last night." Mindy drops her shovel and steps out of the hole as well. "What could it mean, Steve?"

"Not sure." I mull it over in my head. Even the bakery on the corner has a backup generator. It should have fired up by now. "I think I'm going to knock on a few doors."

We finish digging the grave for Frank. I can hardly move. Never been one for a lot of exercise. Now I can hardly lift my arms. It takes all my energy to climb into bed.

Mindy slips in beside me, cuddles up, and my mind goes wild. Do I have a girlfriend? A hot girlfriend? An Asian, hot, girlfriend? The guys on the forums will go wild with this news.

I squeeze Mindy closer and she responds. One leg comes around and she's all of a sudden on top of me. Her hair falls and covers us as we kiss.

We make love. Softly at first, then heat, desire, passion, and the desire to forget the death of someone builds the fury.

I spend inside her and she collapses, all forty kilos of her. Then the tears start again. I keep holding her, stroking her back, hair, giving cooing sound. It works after a while and Mindy slips off me, her back toward me.

A small thought clicks in my head; does she want me to snuggle up or not? You see it on the movies all the time. Man and woman have sex. Woman snuggles to man. If the woman doesn't snuggle to the man, she wants to be left alone. But then again, she may just want me to reach around and hold her. How could I know what she wants me to do? Life, so unfair for the uninitiated.

I struggle. Will she shrug me off? Feel comforted? Reject the intimacy? After what we just did… Decisions. I mentally flip a coin. Flip another. Then realize I've already made up my mind. I roll over and snuggle against her. One arm drapes over and, trying not to hit her breast, rests on her shoulder. Mindy responds by inching against my body. Right move. I feel like a stud, a rock star. Conquer of Worlds.

Her hair still has the wonderful scent of wild flowers about it. Not overpowering, but just enough to notice. Her breathing steadies. I allow myself a mental picture before falling asleep.

Samantha's hiss wakes me. I'm still tangled up with one arm around

Mindy, whose steady breathing tells me she still sleeps, but nothing gets a cat owner going more than the sound of their animal growling and hissing. Even with the night slowly retreating before the morning sun, I can just see her eyes wide, tail puffy, ears flat against her head.

I hear a thud.

The sound makes my bladder scream to be emptied.

Another thud echoes. This one louder, then the sound of a gate being pushed open. Then another thud sounds, followed closely by another. The sound is as if someone is bouncing off the patio door.

I whip off the blankets. Samantha jumps, runs to the head of the bed. She must have hit something tender for Mindy moans and rolls over.

"What's... noise?" She yawns. "What's that noise?"

"Don't know." I pull on pants. "Get dressed, just in case."

Mindy rolls out of bed, throws on some pants as well as one of my shirts, and scoops Samantha up. The cat decides being carried is not in the plans for today. She squirms, backs up, escapes under Mindy's arm. Clawed feet scramble across the bed, hit the floor, and retreat down the hall.

"Damn, I think she got me," Mindy says.

The room is brighter, or I've adjusted to the low light. Either way, I glance over and see a long, red line across Mindy's forearm. No blood.

"Just a scratch." I turn my attention to the bedroom door and force one foot in front of the other.

The thudding gets louder.

A bright light blazes behind me.

"Fuck!" It's a whisper, but still, my voice breaks the monotony of the thudding.

The light goes off.

"What?"

"Okay, wait a sec, my eyes have to adjust." The solid white dot in my eyes start to fade and I swear Mindy is blushing. She puts the flashlight in a pocket and steps beside me.

"I'll be more careful next time." She takes my hand.

"Don't worry." I bend down to kiss her.

There is more than urgency in the kiss. More like a desire to be together. Only two days and the bond is similar to that of the one Samantha and I created when she first came home with me.

Another thud and I end the embrace. "I'll find out what that's all about, then we can figure out what to do today."

She sits on the bed. "Maybe fix up Frank's grave."

I head toward the door. "Yes, that's a good idea."

Mindy follows me out of the bedroom, through the hall, and down the stairs. A quick glance through my octagonal window shows the back gate open.

"We closed the gate yesterday, didn't we?"

Mindy grunts out a positive.

I step up out of the mud room and glance to the kitchen first. A gasp escapes Mindy.

"What's wrong..."

My mind stops working. There is something definitely wrong with the sight we see. I rub tired eyes and step forward. My hand taps the light switch. The backyard floods with illumination. Milky eyes stare through the patio door directly at me without seeing.

Mindy screams as I step back, away from the walking corpse of Frank.

OTHER BOOKS BY DOUGLAS OWEN

The Spear Series
A Spear In Flight
A Sharp Spear Point
Slashed by a Spear Shaft
In Service of the Realm

Coming Soon

The Broken World Series
The Hordes
Biker Family
The Long Walk

Wings
New Wings
Folded Wings
Clipped Wings

Blood Cells
The Awakening of Gregory
Spilled Blood
Blood Infusion

Assassins of Tomorrow
Training Day
In Sight
Trigger Pull
New Clip

Zero-G Series
Rowlinson Inc
The God Drive
Pressed Against the Deck
Turret

Douglas Owen is a writer, author, editor, and publisher. He spends the majority of time behind a computer editing books and stories for his publishing company, DAOwen Publications.

Doug started the writing journey when his interests in adventure games lead him to create many different scenarios for his friends. Later in life he found himself writing training manuals, and teaching two cats how to sit up for dinner.

His interest in reading took him on a roundabout tour of short stories and flash fiction until one friend told him to just write a book. His first work still holds a special place in his heart, but he started publishing with The Spear series. All four YA fiction books were written during NaNoWriMo.

Doug continues to write whenever possible. His fiction can be found online and in many publications.

In 2013, Doug started writing for Self-Publisher Magazine. His entertaining and engrossing series, A Written View, engages new and seasoned writers with advice and information on the writing and publishing world. When the magazine turned into Indyfest Magazine, Doug took over the circulation.

Late in 2014, Doug opened DAOwen Publications and started taking submission. His fingers have been sore ever since.

Doug resides in Goodwood Ontario where he lives with his wife and three well loved cats.